Jason!
  Dude, you are just awesome! ☺
You make working at Wells fun.
Thank you for your support!

DEAD
PROMISE

May all your dreams come true

By: Patch Xiong

INFINITY
PUBLISHING.COM

ISBN 0-7414-5514-5

Cover design by Mike Larsen.

Published by:

INFINITY
PUBLISHING.COM

1094 New DeHaven Street, Suite 100
West Conshohocken, PA 19428-2713
Info@buybooksontheweb.com
www.buybooksontheweb.com
Toll-free (877) BUY BOOK
Local Phone (610) 941-9999
Fax (610) 941-9959

Printed in the United States of America

Published December 2009

Foreword

Dead Promise was inspired by a story my father often told me. As a boy, he bribed me with his many wondrous stories to massage his calves—and it was worth it!

I began drafting *Dead Promise* many years ago as a short story. Then life took a dramatic turn: At twenty years old, I was blamed for the sudden death of my father. Ousted from the house, I bounced from place to place, and with no hope in sight, I ran away from Minnesota to Alaska. Years later, when I lost the "Love of my Life," depression consumed my soul. On that particular night, my knees buckled and I cried on the edge of my bed. I was about to pull the trigger when PaNou, the main character from *Dead Promise*, came to my side and said, "You cannot die. If you die, so will I. The world has to know my story so you must live on. You must keep on writing." Hence, the transformation of a short story into a novel began, and I wrote because I had to; writing gave me life, one sentence at a time. I look back now and I can say this book literally saved my life. When I had no reason to live on, PaNou pushed me forward. Thank you, PaNou!

As you read, please know my intention is purely to tell a story (with minute historical relevance) and not to degrade any government, event, or ethnicity. Additionally, I do not claim any accuracy regarding historical, cultural, or factual references in this novel.

I hope you enjoy reading this book as much as I've enjoyed writing it.

In closing, my personal thoughts about life:

Live life, because life is beautiful. Be kind, because life is so precious.

If you have a dream, do not let anything or anyone stop you. Carry on. When the journey gets most challenging, it only means you are that much closer to the finish line. There are angels along the path. Sometimes you will find them in the least expected places, and sometimes they will find you in the least expected places.

I believe it is better to have tried or failed, then to never. May you stretch the boundaries of your dreams and see where it takes you. You might surprise yourself.

With good wishes,

Patch Xiong
www.patchxiong.com

Acknowledgements

I dedicate this novel to my father, Nhia Thao Xiong, the greatest storyteller, and my mother, Kao Yang, the most amazing woman in my life. She is my every strength and love.

I thank God, the Almighty upstairs. You have spared me so many times from life as a refugee to this very day.

To my family: Thank you for your ongoing support, for believing in me. Our reconciliation was the best turning point, and I would not trade you for anything in this world.

To my friends, acquaintances, and critics: Thank you for your contributions. I believe success is teamwork, and many of these individuals and organizations are listed on the following website:

www.patchxiong.com/acknowledgement.html

Story

PaNou, a young Hmong woman, possessed a very mature appearance for the age of seventeen. She was slender, tall, and her dark silky hair gave her a graceful aura.

Outside of a large wooden house, PaNou shook a flat basket made from woven bamboo strips. Such motion enabled the grains to escape from their hulls. She hummed a romantic hymn about two young lovers who couldn't be together, a favorite from the many her mother sung. A sudden flapping of thong sandals interrupted her tune, and she recognized the large figure.

"Dad…"

Blong had returned from the farm earlier than normal. He tightened his dirty red sash and brushed his sleeves, and he passed without responding. PaNou frowned, then closed her eyes and resumed humming.

"Hurry, let's get going," Blong said, kicking the half-open door so hard it bounced against the wall. He stepped in and immediately began filling his green bottle with water.

"Where are we going?" Youa stopped wiping the table and re-soaked. "I was just about to make lunch."

"We *need* to go to *Dae Lia*."

"For what, Old Man?"

"Stop calling me that."

"I'm just teasing you," Youa chuckled. "Stop being so sensitive." Her complexion changed, and she leered at her husband. "Someone passed away, again?"

"No. Let's get going."

"I'm getting tired of your last-minute ideas." Her eyes flared. She reached for a large knife and waved it as she spoke. "Let's eat first."

PaNou had stopped her work and walked closer to the door to eavesdrop, for it sounded more exciting than their usual conversations.

"I'm going by myself then."

1

"Oh, if it's a second wife you're looking for—"

"Why do you get angry so easily? You know my heart only has room for you."

"Oh, stop that! Aren't you embarrassed if the kids hear you? It's not like we're still dating." Youa looked away to hide her pink cheeks. Then she slid the knife inside its bamboo sheaf.

"You remember Choua Moua?"

Youa cared less and walked to the kitchen for a few enamel plates that looked more like ancient artifacts.

"Tall skinny guy with a big Adam's apple. Remember?"

"No, why?"

Blong scratched his receding forehead. His shoulders dropped. "Okay, when you were pregnant with PaNou and became very ill—at the time we all thought you weren't going to make it. Well, Choua, he was the good friend of mine who brought you the medicine...never mind. You and your short-term memory."

There was a pause. Then smiles blossomed all over Youa's face. "Oh yes, how could I forget. Choua, of course! He gave me that medicine that tasted like cow dung. Even Grandma thought he was crazy."

Blong's eyelids dropped halfway. "It did save your life."

"We never had the chance to thank him, did we?"

"Today's our chance," Blong said. "Pack your stuff and bring some money."

"But isn't he in Thailand? Let's wait until—"

"He's back. Choua's living in Dae Lia now. No one knew until your cousin Ger went to find a wife there and saw him."

"Why didn't you mention this before!"

"Because I just found out this morning. If we stop talking and go now, we can make it back before sunset."

"Right *now*?" Youa disliked leaving chores unfinished. She grabbed a broom made from bamboo branches and began sweeping the heavily stomped dirt floor. "Let's eat lunch first."

Blong made inventory of his basket. He flipped the chicken and rice packs; both were wrapped in layers of banana leaves. "I still have some food from this morning. Just pack us some water. Hurry, let's go."

Youa stared at her dusty black shirt. Its faded red and yellow embroideries on her apron were stained with dirt. She had on a white pleated skirt with a turquoise border decorated with magenta lines and crosshatch embroideries and pleats all around the bottom that was her everyday wear. The only thing presentable was the glowing pink sash. She patted her rear and loosened her sash before walking to the bedroom.

"Let me change first."

"You're a married woman. What you have on is fine." Blong charged out to the dirt road. "We need to get going. Why don't you tell Fong to come also?"

Fong, at fourteen, was the youngest of six. As soon as he heard his name, he raced, scrambling out from his room. Eyes energized, Fong cheered, "Let's go! I'm ready!"

PaNou, already in a bad mood because her father had entirely ignored her, turned her attention to the obnoxious Fong.

"Yeah! I get to go with Mom and Dad." Fong skipped his way past the door and abruptly stopped by the fence. "Mom, can you tell PaNou to clean the house? It's filthy!" He gave his sister a sour-taste look before skipping away.

PaNou cupped her hands over her hips and sneered, "Then clean the house yourself! You have hands, too!"

"This trip isn't for little girls," ordered Blong.

"Little girls?" PaNou's lips tightened. "It's your fault you gave birth to me as a girl."

"PaNou! I don't ever want to hear those words from you again!" Youa shouted.

"But Fong always gets to go. I'm so tired of always staying home."

3

"PaNou!" Blong growled. He pointed his nostrils so high his pupils sunk into his bottom eyelids.

PaNou pursued Fong who dashed past her clawing hands and tumbled. "Fong, you better carry your legs back inside the house."

Fong hopped in circles, excitedly.

"PaNou! Stay home and take care of the house—and make dinner for when we come back," Blong ordered.

"Fong—" PaNou fumed.

"It's too dangerous for little girls. You'll slow us down," Fong responded.

PaNou's eyes lit up like torches. Eyes locked on the younger sibling, she folded back her sleeves and tied her hair into a knot.

Youa added, "My daughter, stay home. You don't want to get your father angry. We're just going to go quickly and we'll be right back."

"I don't care what you all say. I'm going."

"Mom and Dad don't want to baby-sit you," Fong continued.

"I don't have the time to whip the two of you right now." Finished packing, Blong combed his hair, ensuring a perfect line over the left side of his tall head. "All of you, just stay home. If I left earlier I would have been halfway there already."

"Hey, I'm going too!" Youa straightened her hair and stuffed the brush into her basket.

Fong skipped ahead—his black shirt flagging behind him. He stopped in front of his father and stood with a high chin toward the forest.

PaNou charged after Fong who turned his attention to a large shiny beetle on the ground. Her tiny hand snatched Fong's ear and twisted it so hard it nearly turned full circle. Fong squealed. The squeal intensified, and Fong found himself on his knees with one hand twisted behind his back and the other waving angrily.

"Mom!"

"Shut your mouth, Fong!" PaNou said. "This time it's *my* turn."

"Okay. Okay," Fong cried.

Blong swung a bamboo basket over his shoulder and began massaging the side of his face. It was a sign, a sign his patience was running out. "One of you must stay and watch the house." He stampeded away from the house.

PaNou released Fong and rolled back her black sleeves. She then unraveled her jet-black hair, releasing every strand until it dropped to her knees. She slapped the dust off her angel-white skirt that dazzled with multicolored threads and diamond shapes.

Fong ran to his father. "Dad, tell PaNou to stay home!"

"Fong, get back in the house!" exclaimed PaNou.

"You can't tell me what to do." He shook his father's wide trousers to no avail.

"Oh, you're going to eat my fist this time!" PaNou's eyes narrowed.

Youa interrupted, "Fong, my son, listen and stay home. Why don't you let your sister go once? You've gone with us many times before. Be a good son and listen."

"But, Mom—" Fong whined.

"Just go home. Now." Youa's chin pressed against her collar and pointed her finger to the house. "The place we're going is boring. There's nothing to do. Just old people."

"But I—"

"Stay home. When we come back, I'll bring you some lychees—I promise."

Fong began to protest, kicking rocks and flinging his arms wildly.

"Maybe he'll listen to the whip—" Blong grumbled, turning back to the house.

"Fine. Bring me a lot, Mom." Fong picked a rock and slung it at a chicken as it fluttered behind the house.

In that moment, no one was happier than PaNou. She cracked a smile of triumph. A gust of wind lifted the ends of her hair—head high, but not without turning back to give Fong a share of her victory. In response, the envious Fong shouted and displayed his tongue. PaNou giggled and returned him a similar face—a wiggle of the tongue. She trailed behind her parents and as they passed a few houses, they each gave quick hellos to a few elders and a middle-aged woman who was breastfeeding her infant. Then they continued along a neighbor's fenced-in pigs until they reached a narrow but beaten trail that sliced through a grassy field. PaNou fanned the top of the grass while relishing her newfound freedom to travel far from home.

The afternoon weather was perfect with an open sky and cooling breeze. The trail led them straight into the soul of the jungle; its high-pitched chirps combined with low and quick howls formed an exotic orchestra. Suddenly, the village life PaNou had known vanished behind the curtains of branches and sounds as the canopy ate away most of the blue.

She closed the distance with her parents. Afraid she would be sent right back if she mentioned anything, PaNou kept quiet. Her eyes couldn't stand still. They fluttered. Left. Right. Up. Then they steadied into the darker shadows. She tried fighting back, but the horror stories her parents used to tell gradually came to life. From the cavernous darkness and screeching sounds, two were dominant and were similar to the stories her mom told: a deep rhythmic howling cry and a high-pitched buzzing sound. Suddenly, her toe snagged on a root and she went crashing to the ground.

"Nay, nay, what did I say?" Blong stopped and gave his daughter a piercing look. Then he resumed his fast pace.

PaNou rushed to her feet and forced a smile.

An hour later on the trail, the ever-attentive PaNou spied her favorite fruit. "Look, Mom!" PaNou eyed the large ovoid yellow-green fruits, which grew directly from the trunk. Because of three-inch plus thorns on its rind, she slowly and cautiously grabbed between the thorns. With hard but short wiggles, the soccer ball-sized fruit came free. Then she grabbed another. Left. Right. It came off. Then a third one.

"Your younger brother was right. We're really just here to baby-sit you, PaNou." Blong yelled, "Don't you know—those things smell like poop!"

"But they taste the best. And we don't have to pay anything!"

Youa placed her hands on her hips. "Do you realize we still have a long way before we get to Dae Lia?"

"I know, Mom. That's why I'm bringing these. We might get hungry or thirsty." She proudly displayed one of the fruits high on her chest as if it was a trophy.

"As long as you want to carry them." Youa continued walking.

PaNou hastily wrapped the smallest of the three in her sash, securing it back into her waistline. Then she snuggled the other two, one under each armpit.

"Old Man, wait for us!" Youa shouted.

Her shout was answered with a sudden and thunderous rupture from the sky. All the sounds in the jungle came to a halt. The treetops waved back and forth. Hearts frozen, Youa and PaNou looked at each other, while Blong tripped over himself. He spun to one side and struggled back to his feet as he cursed the world. PaNou, who had never seen her father in such an uncharacteristic position, laughed the air out of her lungs, dropping all three durians in the process.

"PaNou! Show more respect toward your father," Youa scolded. Then whispered, "Your father, he's very sensitive—" She tried a straight face but could barely contain herself, and her face wrinkled into laughter.

Furious, Blong ignored the two. He scanned through the small openings of the canopy. Without warning, another thunderous sound sliced the sky, silencing their laughter. The three stood. Observing. They waited but there were no more thundering sounds. Then the jungle orchestra gradually came alive again—layer by layer.

"American A-4!" Blong shouted.

"What's that?" PaNou asked.

7

"Fighter planes. That's why you're still a kid—you don't know anything."

"I *know* they're planes—" PaNou looked away.

"This war is going to get a lot worse before it gets better," declared Blong.

PaNou looked to the sky—mouth wide open. "They're so fast. There's no way the Vietnamese can beat us and the Americans when we have planes like the A...uh A-6."

"A-4 Skyhawk!" He held out four fingers when mentioning the number. "Oh, my daughter, you really don't know anything. The war is not fought up there, and so it will not be won up there. The real fighters are on the land. That's where the war will be won."

"If you know so much, why did they kick you out?" Youa said with sheepish eyes.

"Gosh, if I didn't love you all, I would've left to fight in the war. They would've made me colonel."

"Wow, you actually paid attention in your training," Youa smirked. "Let me tell you something. We Hmong are so stupid, especially the Hmong men. That's why we don't have our own country."

Blong's forehead wrinkled.

"Those Americans. Why would they need us when they have those iron eagles with bombs? They're just using us as puppets—puppets to do their dirty work. I know their plan. They want us to lure the Vietnamese into the jungle and then they start dropping bombs. And all the bomb knows is how to explode. Everything—everyone—dies. Do you think when Mr. Bomb explodes he'll say, 'Oh, it's Blong Lee, excuse me. Please run and hide before I kill the Vietnamese.'" Her piercing stare forced him to look the other way.

He began scratching the hair on the back of his neck.

"Only a mule like you would believe such things. Those Americans don't care about us. All they want is to control the entire world!"

8

"Don't say that. Some of them big-nosed guys are very kind. Some are actually quite funny. Remember when I told you how I met two of them at training camp? They made me laugh so hard I cried. And I didn't even know what they were saying."

"They were probably making fun of you." She then looked at her husband's bulging belly. "If you're ever again a soldier, I'd be Queen ten lifetimes over."

PaNou swayed her head left and right at the exchange between her parents.

Blong breathed in his belly and held it tucked in. "You really don't think I could've been a soldier?"

"A fat man like you—the only thing you can kill is the grass you step on."

PaNou covered her mouth from bursting. Her face was lychee red.

"You don't know because you weren't there. They wanted me. If you don't believe me, ask Lia."

"That opium addict!" Youa pulled her sash. "Let's keep going."

"At least they gave me a rifle and a pistol. They wouldn't give guns to just anybody."

There was no further comment from Youa, and she and PaNou walked ahead. Blong stuffed his pistol back into his basket and readjusted his shoulder straps while collecting whatever was left of his pride.

Shortly afterward, the large fruit was falling from PaNou's sash. She stopped to retie it and wipe her forehead. She undid her sash and stared at the durian. When she looked up, her parents had disappeared around the next turn.

"Wait for me!"

Blong, who was still trying to explain to Youa his reasons for not being a soldier, stopped and looked back. "PaNou. You don't ever listen. Look, each of those weigh ten pounds so that's thirty pounds you're carrying. And for a scrawny girl like you, they must feel like three thousand pounds. Just toss them away now or we'll leave you!"

PaNou's eyes froze on the fruits. She took a deep breath and turned to her mother. Then her arms lowered two away, keeping the lightest one—the one wrapped in her sash.

On the next mile, the trail broke into three paths. Blong knew all three: the left path led to the high hills and the other two led to Dae Lia. The middle one was used often as evident by the centerline of dirt and flattened grass. The right path, however, had trees curved inward, creating a tunnel; it was dark and the tall grass on the trail was uninviting.

"What are you stopping for? You said for us to hurry!" said Youa.

Blong looked neither straight nor right, and instead he peered at the sky. The sun stood a third of the way before setting. He remembered taking the path to the right once many years ago. With treetops blocking most of the sky, it was a dark trail.

"Why don't we just keep going straight, Dad?"

"No," Blong murmured—scratching the bristles on his chin. "This way is faster."

"Let's keep going then," Youa said. "Wait, isn't this the trail you always tell people about when the—"

"Don't be such a kid. I like to dramatize things. Makes it more interesting."

PaNou looked at the shadows and did not move until her parents made their way on to the twisting path between forest and lush foliage. Shortly inside, a particular section of the trail saw trees snuggled together with overlapping canopies. Some trees were swallowed by vines so massive that their once-muscular barks had cringed in mercy. This dense area ranged from the ancient durian to the majestic tualang trees that towered 250 feet high.

PaNou rushed her way in between her parents. On this path, the multiple sounds vanished to two low huffing sounds that worked in unison. PaNou's head bobbed and turned toward the moving sounds until they led her to a pair of enormous trees separated at the ground, but at about ten feet their trunks had merged into one like permanent lovers

10

destined to be together. PaNou's steps slowed and her eyes fell back.

Someone grabbed her collarbone and PaNou flinched to find her mom's mouth widened; it was not to yell but to tell, to tell her something important.

"That, there, is Houa. And that one, that is Saw— cloud and lightning. Like their names, they cannot be without each other." Youa spoke gently behind PaNou's ears while her daughter's eyes examined the odd structure. "But, the Sun and Moon did not allow them to be together."

PaNou lifted her chin to one side.

"You see, a long time ago, the Sun and the Moon were the biggest enemies. Houa was the Sun's daughter, and Saw was the Moon's son. One day Houa was crying so hard in front of Sun her tears created a Rainbow Dragon. She then rode the Rainbow Dragon until it led her to Saw. They disappeared together and had many kids. The Sun and Moon searched endlessly for years, and when they finally found Houa and Saw, the young couple was condemned to be here."

"Is this really them?"

"Yes." Youa returned a slight nod. "That is why every time you see dark clouds, there is lightning. And when it rains, it's because Houa and Saw are weeping for their kids."

PaNou's eyes softened. "But why couldn't they be together? How come—"

"Are you two here to tell stories or to pay thanks to the person who saved both your lives? Without him, there wouldn't be you two loud mouths!" Blong's voice came from around the bend.

Youa waved her daughter forward as PaNou began pestering with questions.

On the next turn, the three entered a different forest where trees were further apart. The terrain was comprised of rises and dips.

"Mom, did you see that?" PaNou pointed at a waving branch.

11

"See what?"

Without warning, the top branches shook violently. Immediately, the noise of broken cries overwhelmed the area like a thousand infants wailing. The three rushed through by covering their ears. A society of small long-tailed monkeys above began to harass them relentlessly. *We must be interrupting their mating season,* thought an annoyed Blong. The shaking of branches and high-pitched screams clanged like the smashing of tin cans. Irritated, Blong hurled anything he could find toward the critters—rocks and sticks flew into the canopy. In retaliation, large nuts began hailing down, many of them at Blong.

"Would you stop the yapping dapping!"

"Dad, they're probably more annoyed with us," said PaNou, skipping and dodging her way through the forest. When the three of them finally passed the monkeys, Blong was the most relieved.

"I should've shot them," said Blong with a firm grip on the pistol. "If they do that again on our way back, we're having monkey soup."

"No thank you!" replied PaNou. The thought of eating monkey made her sick. She had never heard of or was interested in such a delicacy.

"Girls can't eat them anyway."

She looked down at her mother. "Why are there so many things girls *can't* do?"

"Unless you want to grow testicles. It's only for old men."

PaNou's lips shriveled.

"Sometimes not being able to do something is a good thing. Look—your father should be up there with those monkeys. He walks like one."

PaNou ignited in laughter. She'd always known he walked a bit awkward, and finally noticed how his father's toes pointed inward more than normal people. Monkey was the perfect description!

The trail eventually opened up to a flourishing region of banana trees. They treaded slowly, brushing aside the massive green leaves, which curtained their path. Without ever having clear sight of their destination, their journey had felt quite long, particularly to PaNou. The ongoing lectures from her parents didn't help either; each one took a turn while the other one gathered more thoughts.

PaNou breathed, "Can we just relax! I would rather listen to those monkeys back there than you two yelling at me all the time."

"Oh, so you're all grown up now and suddenly don't want to listen."

"Dad—"

"You need to grow up. You're sixteen years old and still arguing with your younger brother. I'm embarrassed for you!"

"I'm seventeen years old."

Blong ignored his daughter and rattled on with life sermons. PaNou was now wishing she never came—for all PaNou could do was tune out and occasionally mumbled, "Erh," to display a submissive response of acknowledgement.

When the trail widened and their shadows began to grow taller, they reached a steep descent. The cliff ahead revealed a breathtaking view: the hundred-foot drop-off opened out to a giant crater-like landscape surrounded by rolling hills stretching upward like green giants. A nearby waterfall crashed against rocks below; its tiny drops fluttered around the cliff like fairies. The angle of the sun's ray created almost a complete rainbow beside the waterfall. In the distance coffee-brown homes scattered throughout the bowl-like basin.

The voice of her father faded as PaNou floated to the edge. It was like a scene from one of her dreams. *Can it be?* She had seen such a place before, but where? PaNou neared the edge and a gust of wind lifted her into serenity. The taste of honey could be discovered in the air. Suddenly, a fierce shout brought her back to earth.

"PaNou! Don't go so close to the edge," said Youa.

In the distance, at the bottom center of the village sat a small pond that was still alive from the last rainfall. The pond radiated a reddish surface like liquid ruby. Her head leaned over the edge.

"What did I just say, PaNou!"

"The water is red!" PaNou took a few steps back.

"That's why this place is called *Dae Lia!*" Blong informed.

"I know, Dad! I was—"

"You talk too much."

The commotion of children came from the village. There was silence among the three. Across the landscape, a thin cloud of blue and green birds flew below them.

"This is so beautiful," PaNou exhaled. Eyes closed, chest elevated, she reached her arms out—catching the breeze into the canals of her sleeves. The gusts danced around her until they bathed themselves into her hair. All was quiet; it was a moment of magic. Then the ruffling of the waterfall returned, erasing the pain from her aching thighs.

"Mom, can we stay here for a little bit longer? Mom?"

No answer. The two had already walked down the path.

PaNou tried to soak in as much of the view as she could, so whenever she closed her eyes it would return. Then, hugging the durian fruit like it was her doll PaNou ran behind her parents into the village.

The many houses looked identical—from the shaggy thatched roofs to the uneven split bamboo slats that formed the windowless walls there were neither street names nor numbers. Identifying someone's house came down to landmarks and visual cues. Finding Choua didn't worry Blong because he could ask around. Most Hmong neighbors knew each other very well. Besides, it had never failed before.

Unlike the lively atmosphere of Lou Sai, Dae Lia possessed a somber emptiness—few adults were out. Small groups of kids sat and played by the dirt road. Another group played a game tossing their thong sandals at an empty can. The rubber thong was folded back to strengthen the rigidity of the sandal before it was tossed. Many of them missed and picked up their sandals, returning to the scratched line on the road for another round. PaNou walked to the group of five: four boys and a girl. They were in their early teens.

"You want to play?" The girl with braided hair asked without looking at PaNou. She was positioning herself to throw.

"Sure!" PaNou picked one of her green sandals.

The girl complained at missing. PaNou folded the strap against the sandal and began circling her arm to loosen her shoulder muscles. With a sharp slice, the sandal's flight was graceful—cutting through the air like a disc until it hit the top of the can so hard the can clanged and bounced.

"Yeah!" PaNou celebrated. It was her first time hitting it on the first throw. She used to play the game with her brothers, but stopped because she never won.

The three boys all turned to look at the new girl in town—jaws dropped.

"You are even better than Toua!" The girl jumped.

Toua, the tallest of the three boys, threw his sandal down and squeezed his foot into it. He blinked slowly and looked at PaNou. "Where are you from?"

"PaNou. PaNou!" Youa shouted.

"Erh, I'm coming."

The girl with the braided hair went back to the game. This time she twirled her arm in circles like PaNou. "Watch this!" It missed.

PaNou and her parents walked toward the heart of the village, between two rows of houses. Without warning, an old man popped out of a shrub and all three of them flinched. His black shirt was left unbuttoned and the left side of the shirt swayed open, revealing crooked lines on both sides of his chest. The old man's hunched back was comparable to

15

one of the enormous hills in the backdrop. As he walked his cane closer, the thin cane he used as a third leg shook anxiously. The senior approached with a wide smile.

"Hello! Hello!" He made tiny and rapid steps. "Welcome! Welcome! My name is..." He looked to the corner of his eyes. "Yes, my name is Nhia Bee Vue. I, I'm one of the village elders here."

"Uh, I can see that," PaNou whispered in response to the old man's claim as a village elder.

"PaNou, close your mouth right now. If you don't know what to say, don't say anything at all. You need to show respect to your elders," Youa said.

Blong and Youa walked to the old man. PaNou wondered if at any second the antique cane would break, sending the old man hurling face first.

Leaning all his weight against the bent cane, Nhia Bee lunged forward with the exertion of the springy cane while reaching out for a handshake.

Startled, Blong focused on the incoming hand. Something caught his eyes that normally didn't. The old man's hands, with thick patches of dried dirt appearing like spots on a leopard were far from clean. Other dark lines resembled streaks of mucus that over time had collected dirt and other debris. Reluctantly, Blong withheld his hand halfway.

This old guy must never wash his hands!

"Welcome!" Nhia Bee gripped Blong's hand. It was a firm and long, very long, handshake.

The elderly man's enthusiasm displayed like he'd been waiting months for their visit. More likely, Dae Lia hadn't seen a visitor for quite some time, for there was nothing fancy about the village that attracted visitors. But things weren't always this way. At one time many people visited, even those from a day's walk away. That was when the pond was much larger—when it actually had fish, lots of fish.

"Come. Come. Let's eat!" Nhia Bee said, nodding his head. He pressed his nose to his wrist, wiping his wet nose.

16

"That definitely was mucus," Blong whispered over to his wife.

"Don't say that so loud."

PaNou giggled.

Blong retrieved his water bottle and nearly emptied it on his hand. Cautiously, they followed Nhia Bee. He would intermittently look over his shoulder and grin. The aged man smiled with countless lines of wrinkles that connected his mouth, eyes, and ears. PaNou, whose skin was wrinkle-free, gawked at the interconnected lines on the old man's face.

Youa distanced herself. "Thank you, but we—"

"I was one of the first settlers in this village," the old man interrupted. "Why, back then, this pond...." He pointed to the approaching pond. "It never dried up before. Now it dries up every year." The old man aimed his cane toward the sky in protest while balancing on his crooked legs. Then he dropped forward with his cane, and continued his gait. "Wait—yes, that's right. The darn pond here used to have fish. Darn biggest fish you'd ever catch in your backyard. That's for sure."

"Really? What's the biggest you caught?" PaNou asked.

"I caught one this big." The elderly man displayed his tiny forearm. "No. This big!" He then stretched his arms as far out as possible, again, balancing on his quivering legs.

"Really," PaNou smiled.

While Nhia Bee debated to himself the fish's true size, Blong and Youa were quietly whispering an exit strategy.

"But ya know what? 'Bout twelve years ago, there was this boy. Yes, he caught a catfish this long! Yes, from the ground up to here...." declared Nhia Bee with one hand pointed to the ground and the other over his head. Knees trembling, Nhia Bee struggled to stand.

Youa returned him a dull stare. Meanwhile, Blong snuck behind their host, fearing he might fall backward.

Nhia Bee eyed Blong, not to question Blong's positioning but to defend his story.

17

"Why, the whole village almost ran away because everyone thought it was a *dragon*. Yep, a dragon! I mean it was enormous!" Nhia Bee nodded rapidly, then paused—looking for an approval from his listeners.

PaNou enjoyed watching as much as listening to the old, yet vibrant man.

"Don't believe me? I was one of them six men that dragged the monster out." He eyed each of the three individually. "I swear to the Sky! You ask any old folk here and they'll tell you the same story."

PaNou fixed her eyes on the pond. Its brownish-red shade was omnipotent. Already, she was lost in the fantasy of such a majestic creature lurking inside the maroon liquid. From the outlining dry bedrock, clearly it had shrunk many times smaller than its original size. Now, the pond was forty feet wide at most.

PaNou and her parents followed the old man—uncertain where they were heading. In short intervals, they watched Nhia Bee's waddling gait. From behind, the elder's bright scalp beamed second in brightness to the sun. His baldness was a desert of skin with exception to a lining of hair behind his ears to the lower back of his head. Abruptly, Nhia Bee stopped, turned to his followers, and smiled wider than ever, displaying his charcoal teeth.

PaNou covered her mouth in repugnance.

Youa slapped her forearm.

PaNou grimaced, holding her burning arm.

"Oh, very sorry—forgot to ask. What's your name? Which village did you all come from?"

"My name is Blong Lee. We're from Lou Sai." Blong rubbed his hands. Initially, he had wanted to introduce himself, but the old man's grubby hands caused him to reconsider.

"Ah, Lou Sai. I hear they have some wealthy folks there." He closed one eye. Smiled. Then nodded and snatched Blong's hand for another solid handshake. "Nice to meet you. You can call me Nhia Bee."

"Yes, you...you told me," said Blong.

Nhia Bee began punching his cane in the ground while turning his attention to the two ladies. "This must be your first and second wife," said the old man, excitedly. "You're a real man—"

Blong grabbed PaNou to display her. "No, this one here—"

"Yes, Blong. You're only one behind me," said Nhia Bee.

With flared nostrils, Youa was ready to snatch the cane and whack the old fart.

"No. No," Blong answered quickly. "This one here..." Blong pushed PaNou forward. "This *here* is my youngest daughter, PaNou. This one over *here* is my wife, Youa."

Such a thought that PaNou was a wife to her father made it difficult to swallow and she shook with disgust.

"Ya know, I don't see the resemblance...maybe the nose, no. Too small. Maybe—"

"Maybe not." Youa was ready to ditch their host.

"Well," Blong intervened, "she looks identical to her auntie."

Youa snarled at Blong.

"Then where's your second wife?" Nhia Bee wrinkled his nose.

"He better not have one," Youa interrupted.

Nhia Bee looked down at Blong, squinting his eyes, studying him oddly for a moment.

"For me, I see it differently. A man only has *one* heart to give. And that's to *one* woman."

Youa dropped her shoulders, and smiled at Blong, though he didn't notice.

PaNou's eyes widened.

Blong began looking across the houses. "Do you know Choua Moua? I heard he—"

"Oh, ya know Choua Moua?" The old man lifted his left brow, which folded half a dozen more lines.

"Yes, you know him? Where's his house?" Blong asked.

PaNou fixed her sash and hair while they conversed. Then, tiny ripples on the red pond stole her attention. A few bubbles surfaced and popped. The shimmering waves silenced the voices around her.

"Hey—" PaNou pointed, but no one cared to listen.

"Choua," Blong said, "He and I, we go way back. We grew up together in Panasavong."

"Ya know, if it's the Choua you're talking about, he's been here for years. He doesn't talk much."

"Yeah, he is a bit shy. If I'd known he was in Dae Lia, I would've come here sooner."

Their host altered his head and began taking a few loud sniffs. "Ahhh. Smells delicious! My wife just finished making supper. Why don't you all come over and we'll chat some more?"

"Hey, look—" PaNou jumped, entranced and excited at the fizzling bubbles while her parents and Nhia Bee chatted, unaware.

Some children heard her and they began congregating near the pond; one threw a rock into the pond. The bubbles continued popping. PaNou tossed a few pebbles in.

"We ate before coming so you go right on ahead," Youa smiled, forcibly.

"Well, I tell ya! Chicken leg is the best! Oh, you must come and try my wife's pepper. It's very good."

"Choua lives here, right?" Blong asked again.

"Who?" Nhia Bee frowned.

"Choua." Blong grew increasingly edgy. If Nhia Bee were younger than Blong, he would've spanked him a lifetime ago. Now Blong just wanted an affirmation that Choua really was in Dae Lia.

"Oh, you worry too much. That guy could never get lost if he tried. I can't believe a good man like you is a friend of that smelly guy. I say, smells as strong as the chicken my wife's making—but it's certainly not something you want to eat." Nhia Bee grinned and smeared a line of mucus on his wrist. "Maybe I shouldn't have said that. Not very polite of me, ya know."

Blong turned to his wife to find a reason not to smack the old man. If they had searched on their own, they might have already found Choua. Youa raised her shoulders and lightly shook her head sideways, pressing her husband to stay calm and patient.

"He smells that bad?" Blong responded—not remembering his friend as someone with bad hygiene. *It must be a different Choua he's talking about.*

"Yep, smells like rotten fish mixed with lime. Just *nasty*, I tell ya," Nhia Bee said. "Oh, this is killing my appetite."

"Choua Moua. This is Tong Moua's son, right?" Blong asked.

"Don't know. Like I said, he doesn't talk much." Punching his cane in the ground, Nhia Bee resumed, "Let me see, there was something he warned me to not do...must not be important—"

"Come eat right now!" A woman with a coarse voice yelled from a few houses away.

Nhia Bee waved his left hand forward and began walking toward his house. "C'mon. Don't be shy. The day is long. Come and let's eat! We have lots to talk about."

"Thank you, but—"

"We're all the same Hmong. Bring your two wives over."

"That's my *daughter*." Blong pointed to PaNou. Blong breathed heavily because his tank of respect was running empty. Annoyed, Blong couldn't determine if the old man was partially deaf or suffered from dementia.

"Why so shy? Let's eat!"

Blong groaned, "Sir, thank you, but perhaps next time. It's urgent I talk to Choua." He looked to his wife to play along.

"Yes, it's really good news we bring," Youa nodded. "We must let him know right now."

"That's good." Nhia Bee stopped. He looked to the ground momentarily. "He needs it. He hasn't come out for weeks. Who knows if he's still alive in there?" Nhia Bee turned around. "You see that dried tree back there?" The old man pointed half a dozen houses behind them. Over the roofs they saw the top of a tree with most of its branches sagging.

"I see," Blong growled.

"We walked past it, and you didn't even—" Youa fired back.

"Next to that tree is a large rusty tin can. Choua's house is next to it."

PaNou who had walked back to the pond was content that she was now in front. Many more local kids had joined her in observing the bubbling surface. They circled the pond. She began cutting the durian fruit into pieces and handed most of them to the children. The kids pushed their way in only then to quickly race away with pinched noses.

"Ehhww...smells like poop!" A boy warned the others.

PaNou giggled, "You should try it though. It's very sweet."

A little girl tugged PaNou from behind. Sucking two fingers, she tugged again looking at the durian. Her uneven bangs covered her entire right cheek. She was at most ten years old. Her other hand clung on to an old doll that looked like a Cabbage Patch Kid; its hair had fallen off from constant braiding and its dress had been torn off. One of the eyes didn't open.

"Hi, what's your name?" PaNou asked.

The little girl shrugged her shoulders and stopped sucking her fingers. Then a taller girl with a large smile stretching from ear to ear approached.

"Her name is Dumbhead," laughed the tall girl.

"Hey! Don't call her that!" PaNou scorned. Her eyes darkened and the girl walked away. PaNou squatted to set the durian pieces aside and held the small girl by the shoulders. "Won't you tell me your name?"

Her shoulders lifted—then dropped.

"Here, I will give you all of this if you tell me your name."

A mumble came from the girl. PaNou slowly pulled the girl's fingers out and a slimy red string stretched and dangled. The little girl turned away and ran, but PaNou gripped her wrist. In the quick tussle, the girl dropped the doll and its head popped off—rolling and rolling into the shallow waters of the orange pond. Blood trickled from both her mouth and fingers.

PaNou turned to look at the girl, eye to eye. "What happened? Why's your mouth bleeding?"

"They...beat my hand."

"Who?" PaNou looked around. "Where's your mom? I'll take you to your mom."

"My mom is up there." The girl looked to the sky.

PaNou's chest dropped. "And your dad?"

"He's up there with my mom."

"Do you have any brothers or sisters?"

The little girl nodded and ran to the edge of the pond and retrieved the head. She twisted it back on the neck and displayed the doll like it were a new toy again, and smiled, "This is my sister, Kabao."

PaNou tightened her sash and knelt down. Then a gust of wind blew the side of the girl's bangs, and PaNou noticed something. "Can you come closer for a second?" The little girl walked forward. PaNou brushed her bangs aside—revealing a closed eyelid. The color was a bruised violet. It had difficulty opening. PaNou looked at the doll's face then to the girl's.

"Kabao loves me a lot. She didn't want me to be the only one."

PaNou inhaled a deep breath, and replied, "Who did this to you?"

"They beat my hands with a stick. They..." The girl's hands shook fiercely. Then she dropped Kabao.

PaNou held the girl's ragged sash, and then tore a strip off. With her own sash, PaNou wiped the blood clean from the girl's fingers and mouth. In a minute, she wrapped the strip around the girl's bleeding fingers.

"Food is ready!" A woman's voice interrupted. "Why, when there's food, no one wants to eat, and when there's no food, everyone's complaining I don't cook. I don't care! First come. First serve!"

PaNou turned to the shouting woman. At that instant, the girl snatched the largest piece of durian and ran, and she handed the piece to the tall girl who had called her Dumbhead earlier. PaNou stood, watching for a moment. Then she walked to the pond and washed the blood off her hand. The girls had made it to the other side of the pond.

"You keep doing that, and I'll be your friend!" said the tall girl.

A dust devil blew through the remaining pieces of durian. PaNou brushed her face and looked to the blood-stains on her sash. She soaked and rubbed it, but the blood didn't come off. Then the chatter of Youa, Blong, and Nhia Bee grew again.

"After you're done talking with Choua, you must come visit me!" The old man swung his shoulders to dash like a gazelle, but instead he crawled like a tortoise—head lunging out as far as his neck permitted.

Kids and teens from between, behind, and inside other houses flooded Nhia Bee's house. PaNou and her mom noticed the river of children.

"Eight, ten...wow *sixteen* kids," said PaNou.

"No. Seventeen," Youa corrected. Instantly, a young girl, old enough to run hurried to the house, stumbling forward.

"Seventeen kids! Is that even possible?" PaNou knew it was possible, but she couldn't imagine herself bearing so many.

"Sure it is, especially with three wives," answered Youa as she stared crossly at Blong—eyebrows frowned in a "V" and lips shrunk into a moth. It was a "If you know what's good for you, don't you dare marry a second wife" look that Blong was fully aware of.

24

"Hey, wonder how Choua's doing?" Blong marched onward.

The three made their way to the leaning teak tree. A large rusty tin can sat between two similar-sized houses. With the can's ancient body mired into the soil, flies zipped in and out of a small opening at the side. As Blong passed the can, a few flies trailed him.

The houses resembled abandoned sheds, yet one was completely different from the others—the one to the right had a few spaces between the bamboo splints big enough to stick one's head inside. The left one had so many layers of bamboo it could easily be mistaken for a giant pile of bamboo if not for its door. Blong looked back and forth a few times before turning to his wife.

"Well," Youa asked, "which one smells worse?"

Blong scanned around to ensure no one was watching. He then walked to each house and sniffed the air.

"I didn't mean for you to literally sniff it..." Youa covered her face.

"I can't believe Dad's actually doing that," PaNou said, looking away and rolling her foot over a rock. "Let's go back and ask that old man and—"

"Unless you want to be his fourth wife, I don't *ever* want to see that Nhia Bee again."

"Okay, Mom. So then why don't we just knock?—"

"This one," Blong proclaimed, with his nose pointing.

Blong approached the house to the right of the tree. The two followed him to the door, which was ajar. There inside, Cheng, a young man in his early twenties, was home alone—frantically scrubbing a pan. A portion of his shirt fell over his arm. His tattered shirt was secured in front by one large button where three others were missing. Cheng threw his left shirt over his shoulder and repeated this each time it fell. His shaggy hair swung left and right with the scrubbing. Occupied, Cheng didn't notice the man standing at the door until Youa pushed the door wider to see who was inside, which caused the top door hinge to break from the rotting door. Blong grabbed the door before it fell and pressed it against the inside wall. Startled, the young man jumped to his feet with a deer-in-the-headlights stare.

"Who are you?" Blong asked. He knew the man was too young to be Choua. Maybe he was Choua's son.

"My name is Cheng...is there something I can help you with?" Cheng found it rude for a visitor to walk into someone else's house demanding their name.

Blong continued, "Are you Choua Moua's son?"

"No..." Cheng dropped the aluminum pan. The wet pan was now covered with dirt and he set it in the large bowl of water to rewash it.

"Why are you not washing outside?" Youa asked.

Cheng didn't answer. He looked concerned and worried.

"Choua Moua...does he live here or not?"

Cheng looked up at Blong. "I don't know. I think he's next door."

Blong nodded, then reached out his comb and quickly reconfigured his thinning hair to the side.

Youa dropped her head to the side. "Old Man, you're here for what—to find a girlfriend?"

"Hey, it's been a long time since I've last seen him."

"I'll go next door and check," said PaNou.

"No. We'll go together," replied Youa.

Cheng paused. To his amazement, two smooth legs walked out from behind Blong and Youa. Soft toes, perfectly inserted into candy-green sandals, followed by bright multicolored panels on a snow-white skirt drifting across the dirt floor. The perfect texture of two slender calves dazzled the limits of Cheng's sight. Her figure came into view as Blong and Youa made their way out.

Cheng's face brightened and his heart galloped. *Wow!*

Blong stepped back, blocking PaNou. "You live here and you don't even know your neighbors? Who is your father?"

Cheng looked past Blong. PaNou came in full sight, talking to her mom. The young man's eyes crawled from her thin ankles, up her curves, and then, he caught a glimpse of her face—a light peach color with seductive lips he never knew existed. Hunger and all the stresses of poverty vanished. Instantly, Cheng lost grip of the pan, and it rolled across the dirt floor between Blong's legs, spinning around until it sat beside PaNou's ankle.

PaNou stopped at the middle of her sentence. She knelt down and picked it up. On her way up, she tucked her shimmering black hair behind her left earlobe. PaNou brought the pan across the room and set it in front of Cheng. She didn't look at him until her last finger left the pan—a quick smile.

Angry at the young man's rudeness, Blong jumped in, retrieved PaNou, and quickly shoved his family outside. In a flash, the visitors were gone.

Cheng stared at the rim of the pan that PaNou had touched. He looked up, and then realized how rude he was. *I didn't even say "thank you" to her!* He placed the brush inside the pan and rushed to the door. He stepped out. His eyes fastened on the long hourglass figure of PaNou: firm shoulders with perfect hips bouncing left and right.

Cheng massaged his dry cheeks and pounded dirt off his pants. The young woman's long silky hair danced all the way down to her knees. Something about her energy was so strong it transfixed him. Suddenly, the world was showered with butterflies. He swallowed a deep breath, and with a heavy foot outside, Cheng pulled his pants higher and tightened his loose sash. He licked his fingers and began fixing his unruly thatched hair.

In awe, all the young man could do was pray that she'd notice him. Swiftly, PaNou spun her head and caught him eye to eye. Her sharp almond-shaped eyes of perfection pierced his heart. She smiled. Cheng froze—then looked away to hide his embarrassment. When he looked up, he found two angry eyes instead—PaNou's mother. Cheng jumped inside the house.

"This village has so many rude people," said Youa.

"That boy needs to be taught manners," Blong muttered and began knocking on the door. He turned to PaNou. "When we go in there, don't talk so much. Close your mouth and listen."

PaNou rolled her eyes.

The picture of PaNou's radiant smile tattooed Cheng's mind. He kept his eyes shut to relive that moment—small sharp nose, brows that rainbowed over her eyes, and ruby lips. No one could take that away from him. As he held his hands against his chest, a large smile warmed his heart.

Blong gave the door a few good knocks. Finally, the door creaked an inch inward. Yet, all they could see was an eyeball peering at them. Then a cloud of rotten smell enveloped them. PaNou pinched her nose with a scouring look. The air smelled exactly like how the old man had described: rotten fish sauce mixed with lime. Suddenly, Nhia Bee wasn't so much a lunatic as Blong had thought. To not disrespect the stranger behind the door, Blong and Youa maintained their tolerance.

"Hello." Blong cleared his throat. "Does Choua Moua live here?"

"He moved out years ago." The voice was shaky and quick. "What do you want with him, anyway?"

"Will he be back soon?"

"Don't know. He's not here." The door slammed shut.

"I don't ever want to come back to this village again," Youa complained. "The Hmong here are so different."

Disappointed, Blong looked over his shoulder to his wife. He puffed, "Well—"

"We should've never listened to Nhia Bee," Youa said.

Blong sighed. He looked to his wife, then to his daughter. The rays of the sun were beating on his balding scalp, so he stepped into the shadow of the house—thinking. Youa watched. With a determined look, Blong headed back to the door and knocked again. "Hey, if you see Choua, can you please tell him his old friend Blong came to see him?"

No answer.

Blong felt like kicking the door but instead, stared angrily at the shut door. Youa pulled him by the arm.

"Let's go home. I'm getting hungry."

The two started walking.

The door opened halfway.

"Blong. Blong Lee from Lou Sai?"

Upon hearing his name, Blong stopped and faced the house. Rubbing his eyebrows quickly, his eyes narrowed, focusing on the shadowy figure from the house.

Youa pulled Blong's arm to leave, but he stood firm.

"Choua?"

"Blong! Is that really you? And Mrs. Blong! I almost didn't recognize you two." The door opened completely. A scrawny and bent figure came into the light. His once-white shirt was permanently gray from years of being unwashed. The man wore a thin but long beard that twirled into a hook at the tip. He possessed the face of a ruined man—one eye hung lower and was smaller than the other, and a smile required all the muscles in his body. "Huh, you packed on even more meat."

"Choua! It's so good to see you! So, *finally* we meet again!" Blong grabbed Choua's thin figure and gave him a bear hug until his thick odor stopped him. Blong held his breath.

"Come. All of you in the house."

"PaNou!" Youa called.

The inside had a dusty darkness. It was simple: an empty square space with scattered strips of branches, some pots and plates, and a pile of dried grass. There was no table to dine on—just two handmade wooden chairs. Cobwebs hung across the corners. Black pants with one leg spliced in rags dangled on the opposite wall.

Choua handed Blong the wider of the two chairs. "Have a seat."

PaNou stopped at the door, looking back at where the children were playing. She fingered her hair behind her ears and looked outside and inhaled a long breath of fresh air.

"Come inside and close the door," Choua demanded.

PaNou walked in and looked at each corner of the tiny house. Although small, it had multiple layers of bamboo splints. Tiny rays of light streamed from the west wall. Once the door closed, their eyes adjusted to the darkness.

"So you got a second wife," Choua gleamed. "But I have to say, I'm a bit surprised. Everyone knew you as the man with one heart, one wife. "

PaNou covered her head in abhorrence.

Blong shook his head in frustration, forcing a wide smile. "This is my youngest *daughter*, PaNou. You remember her—" He paused, then corrected himself, "Oh, of course not. She was only a baby then. But she and my wife are well because of you."

"She's certainly grown a lot," Choua admired. "Love your mom very much. You must remember your mom nearly lost her life giving birth to you. And now look at you—you're almost as tall as your father." He stared at her. "PaNou...that's a beautiful name."

"Thanks, but I don't really like my name. It's too girly."

"Well, I bet your house must have a line of men outside every day."

Embarrassed, PaNou hid behind her hair. "My dad shot one."

"I didn't hit anyone. Just to scare them away. They need to respect our privacy," Blong said. "I don't want *any* man to marry my daughter. Besides, she's still immature. Maybe another year. She still has a lot to learn to be a good housewife."

"Sometimes they don't grow up until they are married." Choua smiled, nodding his head while he twirled his beard.

"What's with the long beard, my friend?"

"Blong, you never change. Always asking about one's appearance first before how one is." Choua stretched his arms back. "Life has been too busy. I wanted to ask you about *that*." Choua remarked at Blong's hanging belly. "Though you got pregnant, you haven't aged at all. You have to tell me, what's the secret?"

They all broke into laughter, but PaNou's laughter dominated them all.

Blong cupped his drooping belly. He looked at it and chortled, "Eat a lot! That's the secret." Realizing he was only sucking in more of Choua's nasal-clogging smell, Blong stopped laughing. "So, how long have you been hiding here?"

"How'd you know I was hiding?" Choua's face darkened. The smile died out, revealing grave fear. He rose and looked through a hole in the wall.

"Oh, I was just saying—" Blong replied.

Choua took a long breath. He looked chalk white like his spirit was suddenly taken.

"It's been a long time since I've heard a word from you. Don't take this wrong, but I really thought you were dead."

"In a way, I did die. A lot of things have happened. I lost track of time…lost everything." Choua found his way back onto the stool.

Youa's brows depressed. "What do you mean?"

With a somber look, Choua ran his hands forcefully through his frizzled beard, spinning the tip of it. He began scratching his forearm hard. The nails on his hands were dark and chipped.

Blong looked to his wife, signaling her with the wink of his brows. "We brought this for you. It's long overdue."

Youa shrugged her basket to one side and reached forward a large black bundle. She handed it to Choua whose arms lowered with the weight of the bag. Choua looked at them and back at the bag. He studied it nervously.

"It isn't much, but it's from us." Blong continued, but seeing how much larger the bundle was, his expression glowered.

"Choua," Youa spoke, "we would've given it to you sooner, if we knew you were living here."

Choua squeezed his eyes at first to decipher what the gift was. His breathing—heavy and slow. He looked directly at Blong. Choua now knew what it was, and was fearful, not of what was in the bag, but something else. Eyes widened. "How'd you know I was here?"

"You're sweating like the Vietnamese are after you," Blong said, humorously.

"That stupid old man told you, didn't he?" Choua didn't find it amusing. "Hmm."

Blong turned his confusion to his wife.

PaNou interrupted, "You're talking about Nhia Bee? He was really funny—"

"I should kill him. That stupid old man," Choua whispered. "Now they're coming. Soon, they'll find me."

"Who's coming? Nhia Bee?" PaNou found it comical.

Blong gave his daughter a heavy eye. "Who is after you?"

"Those Communist devils!" Choua jumped toward the door and made sure it was shut. Then he quickly tied the end ropes of the door against the wall. "That old man doesn't remember anything. I told him not to tell anyone. I'll have to kill him first."

He's even crazier than that old man, thought PaNou.

Tired of waiting for Choua, Blong opened the bundle. Part of it was his own aching curiosity of how much his wife had actually brought.

"*Six* silver bars!" Blong yelled—surprised. He then caught his rudeness and covered it up with a smile. "Yes, here are six silver bars! All for you, Choua."

"Why so much?" Choua grabbed each bar, feeling the hard and smooth surfaces, and laid them on the ground. It

32

was difficult to tell from his tone if he was content or distressed. He slumped lower.

Blong took notice of the back end of an M-14 exposed under a rag behind Choua.

"You joined the Americans. Didn't you?" Blong asked.

Choua followed Blong's eyes to the rifle. He reached over and held the weapon on his lap. "No. I joined General Vang Pao."

"Why do you fight in the war?" PaNou asked.

"Ah, why are you so dumb? Now keep your mouth close and listen," Blong reminded.

Youa leaned forward. "These last few days and even on our way here, there are more and more American planes flying over us. They're flying from the west and they're dropping bombs everywhere—"

"That's good. I hope they kill every single one of those Communists! I hope the Americans bomb them all to hell."

Youa sat back, appalled.

"Why do you hate them so much?" PaNou asked.

"You see, both the Lao and Vietnamese Communists, they have no respect for us Hmong. They treat us like animals. Before the war even started, they forced us to pay taxes because they said we were using their land.

"They destroyed our crops, raped our women, and murdered our children." Anguish evoked from Choua's voice. "Why? Because *we're* Hmong, and as long as you and I are Hmong, they'll kill all of us. Then, when the Americans told us they'll help get our country back if we fight with them against the Communists, that's when General Vang Pao joined, and that's why I fight. It's time to show them that we Hmong are fierce and strong. And you, Blong—why aren't you fighting?"

Blong sighed, and hesitated to find the best reason.

"It's been hard for him, Choua. He didn't have the heart to leave me and his family alone, so he came back."

"But Mrs. Blong, it is our people who are being killed out there." Choua pointed the rifle toward the door. "Our brothers and sisters are dying while we sit here. You know what? We shouldn't sit here for too long either, because they'll come through every village, find us, burn our homes, and slaughter every single one of us."

Blong cleared his throat, and responded, "We are fighting. Maybe not with guns, but someone needs to pack and send food and medicine to our Hmong soldiers. Every day, we're doing that."

"Hmmm." Choua had much to counter Blong's reason but decided not to. He then turned to the silver bars. "This is too much. I won't know what to do with it."

Blong and Youa smiled. Looking around the empty house, Youa eagerly advised, "You need a table to eat. More chairs. New clothing—"

"In times of war, these things mean nothing." He paused. Choua looked around his dark, quiet house.

"Choua, we never had the chance to say 'thank you' to you. We are forever indebted to you. Because of you, my wife and daughter are alive today." Blong's eyes glimmered. "Also, I still remember many years ago you helped me when the Her Clan sued me because of my oldest daughter's trouble with them. At the time, I had nothing, but you paid them with your two cows.

"From that day on, I told myself I was going to make sure my family had a good life, a good name. I'm now making money as an advisor to the mayor of Lou Sai and other villages. I also work as a Lao and Thai translator," Blong said. "My wife here makes good money selling herbal medicine. So please, don't feel bad taking this. It's a small token for all your help."

"No need to say that. Friends help each other and never ask for anything back."

"Please take this. It'll make me feel better. Plus, it's something to get you by."

There was silence.

Blong smiled, "Friends help friends out, right? If there's anything else I can do, you have to tell me. If you don't tell me then how can I help you?"

"I believe everyone has two hearts. One is pure and warm. The second is evil and cold. If you don't look after the warm heart, it too can do the work of evil."

Blong and Youa listened attentively to the change of tone. PaNou wanted to say something but saw the warning on her father's face and she bit her lips together.

"What do you mean?" Youa asked.

With his hands, Choua smudged his face. "I'm not the Choua you once knew. I've changed. After the two cows I gave you, what was left of my livestock was all stolen. At the time my first wife and I were at your house while my second wife and children were all home. That day, on the way back home I noticed the door was wide open. Dishes and silverware—all gone. Everything except the walls and roof."

"My goodness," Youa said with her mouth left open. She combed her hair over her right chest, thinking about her own house—hoping Fong and the house were fine. "And your family, we heard some tragedy happened."

Choua stopped to gather his thoughts. While he spoke, he stared into space as if he were watching a film. "I looked for my children first but no one was inside. The place was a mess like a tornado had blown through it. Then, I saw dark red stains on the ground that trailed out of the rear door into the backyard. Maybe it was chicken or pig blood, I thought...

"When I went out to the back I saw..." Like a sudden downpour, Choua broke into tears. His fingers dug into the rifle. Choua clenched his teeth and was about to claw his face. "...their heads—impaled on sticks."

Blong rubbed his friend's shivering shoulders.

"Those devils. They killed my entire family. They were just kids." Choua sobbed. "My life changed forever. I had nothing left. Nothing! When I learned that some of those devils lived in Thailand, I went after them. I had to find

35

those murderers and make them *pay* for what they did." Choua held fists to his chest.

Blong's eyes reddened and he began sobbing. It was the first time PaNou had ever seen her father break down.

Choua had the glaze of a broken soldier.

"I'm so sorry, my friend."

"It's not your fault. No person with heart would kill children. Since that day all I wanted to do was to kill every single one of them—their brothers, cousins…everyone." He stopped to breathe. "I suppose it must be my fate, written on paper to be this way."

Youa covered her mouth—speechless. Blong's eyes were soaked with guilt. Suddenly, the six silver bars seemed worthless—nothing more than rock from earth.

"Did you ever find them?" PaNou asked.

"I did. I-I killed three of them. And one, I killed him and his wife in front of their own children. But I, I wanted to, but I couldn't kill their kids. I saw my own kids in their eyes." Choua spoke, looking stoically at the ground.

Both PaNou and Youa covered their faces in horror.

"For a while, they thought I ran back to Laos, but no, I hid in Thailand for many years and came back here a year ago. From that day on, they've killed more Hmong families at random, saying we're a bunch of rebels out to take over their government. It's no excuse for them to keep killing us. We have no rights here. We're not even humans to them. We have no option but to fight or be killed."

Blong cracked his knuckles. "When I hear these things, I want to pack my rifle and kill them all—"

"War isn't the answer. If you kill their children, they too suffer like us, Old Man," Youa said.

"Stop calling me 'Old Man.'"

"So why don't you keep hiding in Thailand?" PaNou asked.

"They found out where I was in Thailand. I know I can't hide forever. Everyone dies one day. When they come, mark my words, I'll kill at least one more."

"Why don't you settle down, Choua? There are many single women in our village," Blong said.

"Have you ever killed anyone? Have you killed someone with your hands, and you can see life escaping through his eyes?"

Blong slightly shook his head sideways.

"Good. Once you do, you're never human again."

Youa wiped heavy tears under her chin, and held her husband's hand. "Choua, I know it's very difficult because they took your family away from you, but by killing another family how will this ever end? Until everyone dies?"

"All I know is, if we don't kill them, they'll keep on killing us. So why not kill them first." Choua possessed eyes with no soul and used his hands vibrantly as he continued, "On one night, I saw the bravest Hmong soldiers. We were awakened by an explosion—then it was nonstop gunfire. Bullets screamed everywhere." His eyes fluttered toward the ceiling. "They, they protected me and told me to run. I kept running and running, but my heart wanted to go back and fight with them. I ran and ran until I just fainted." He took a heavy breath. "Now, I feel shame hiding in this village."

"When I was in training, the Americans instructed us not to fight in Thailand. So I understand why you hid there for so long. It was the best place," Blong added.

"I'll keep on fighting. I have nothing left anyway—nothing to live for." Choua closed his eyes. "War is like poison."

"That is it." Youa was growing irritated at the atrocity of fighting. "War *is* a disease. They inflict it on you and now you're inflicting it on them. And then it never stops—until everyone dies."

"Choua," Blong interrupted and held his hand up, "I hope you know how much we appreciate you—"

"All of this was written on our *paper*, our destinies. Blong, you know that." Choua squeezed each bar before laying them on the open floor. He grabbed a hoe with a broken stick and began digging. Blong and Youa watched curiously. Choua carefully set each bar side by side like tiny coffins and buried them.

"That's a good idea," said Blong, thinking he should do the same to hide his savings.

Choua gave no eye contact.

Youa paid more attention to Choua's facial expression than his digging. "You don't want it?"

"What does money mean when you have no one to share it with?"

There was a long pause. The rest of their conversation was somber and continued into the evening. Blong wanted to leave so the three could be back before nightfall, but found it difficult to cut their conversation.

"It is wonderful to see you again, my friend. It is getting late," said Blong.

Then the worried Choua pressed, "I'm sorry. If I was thinking straight, I should've not let you all stay in here for this long. This is not a safe place."

The entire time, Cheng stood inside his house, back against his door. The serenity of love inflated his lungs. In his twenty-three years, Cheng's heart, mind, and body had never once blossomed so abundantly. He returned to his corner, rubbed his forehead and picked up a large cleaning brush, the one he stole from a neighbor. A scrub became a burden. Boring. Too much effort. Unable to do anything else, Cheng clanked it inside the pan.

On his way out of Choua's house, Blong smiled, "You must come visit me soon."

"If it is written on my paper, then perhaps. If not, I wish you and your family well."

"We'll be forever indebted to your kindness."

"Blong, don't say those words. We help each other out."

"All right, my friend. Be safe, and if I were you, I'd get out of this village." Blong looked at him straight in the eyes. "I will see you again, maybe in Lou Sai."

"If not, in another lifetime."

"We'll *meet* again."

"Choua, thank you. We'll see you around. Please take care of yourself," Youa added. She immediately whispered to PaNou, "Why are you so stupid—go thank the man. If not for him, there wouldn't be you."

"But Dad told me to be quiet and—"

Youa tilted her head.

PaNou rushed to Choua and held his leathery hands. "Thank you very much. If you didn't help my parents, there wouldn't be me. Thank you."

Choua nodded. He cupped PaNou's hands and kissed them, and smiled, "Soft hands. Soft heart." He flipped her hands to read her palm. His eyes propped open. "Listen well. This line breaks into two: one is short and straight, the other long and uneven. You have two destinies—choose your husband carefully. See, this one will love you completely, but it will be short-lived. This other one will abuse you, but you will live to be a very old woman."

"Erh," she nodded.

He stepped back into the shadows of the house.

When the clapping sandals of PaNou's footsteps grew faint, Cheng lifted the door open and crouched out. *What if I never see her again?* Cheng set his hands on his hips, pondering. Then he looked out to the darkening sky. Three figures disappeared behind a row of homes. With a slight nod to himself, he closed the door behind him, and followed the visitors. He used every minute of his experience as a young boy hunting with his father—from chasing squirrels to wild boars. And though he hated the act of killing, he enjoyed the process of stalking very much. Never in his wildest imagination had he thought such hunting ability would ever be practical. Until now.

Cheng listened to each footstep. He became the master hunter his father taught him—prowling after the visitors like the biggest trophy hunt. He maneuvered behind trees, through tall grasses, and into dense jungle. At times, he crawled on all fours, walked on his knees, sat quietly, and sprinted with long soft strides. And in the process he kept enough distance so they never suspected being followed. All went well until a tree root snagged Cheng's foot, hurdling him into some bushes. Cheng tried rolling out of the fall to defuse as much of the noise as possible.

Bam! Bam! Without warning, two shots were fired.

PaNou jumped and was speechless—eyes glued to the high pistol.

"Are you insane?" Youa grabbed her chest, breathing heavy and loud. She retightened her sash, and stopped when she saw swaying bushes in the distance.

Cheng crept next to a large fallen tree blanketed with fungi.

Arms spread apart, Blong ducked low and walked back down the trail. "Stay here and don't say a word."

PaNou hid behind her mom who crouched as low as possible. The air was damp. Blong broke a cold sweat. His heart—pounding like a drum. His rusty pistol led him nervously forward. Blong stopped two times to scan the trees and plants before him. There was no sound except the flutter of swaying leaves and birds whistling throughout the canopy.

Blong turned around to find his daughter and wife's faces directly behind him. Startled, Blong fired another shot into the canopy.

"What are you doing?" Youa yelled, as quietly as possible.

"You two, stay back!" Drenched in sweat, Blong closed his eyes—breathing heavily.

"Give *that* to me." Instantly, she snatched the gun from Blong's grasp.

"You made me waste a bullet. Now there's only one left."

"Good! I might need to use it on you." Youa set her basket down and walked toward the moving leaves.

Blong's forehead fell back in dismay.

She snooped around—then disappeared into a thick area of large plants. For a nerve-pounding moment, Blong and PaNou waited. PaNou had found a sharp stone and held it firmly—in case. The tops of the bushes began to sway. PaNou and her father treaded forward.

Youa emerged. "There's nothing! Why, you should marry that crazy old man Nhia Bee."

"Have some respect for your husband," Blong said.

"Look." Youa dove inside bushes and popped back, revealing a bright red fruit. "I've never seen any lychee this big!" She went back to the bushes and stuffed as many as she could inside her sash. "And I completely forgot about bringing Fong lychees."

Blong, meanwhile, looked cautiously around them. A yard from Youa, Cheng lay flat at the bottom of a dip—motionless in the shadow. Her loud voice hovered over him and she picked her way closer, and closer. Cheng didn't breathe. His mind screamed for a miracle.

"It's getting dark. Let's get out of here."

"Yes, Dad," PaNou agreed. "Mom, let's go. Please? I don't think I'm going to come next time."

On their way back to where the monkeys had harassed them previously, the loitering was absent. The monkeys had relocated to a different hillside, likely due to Blong's protest from before. The sun was now sitting low and the shadows darkened the area. Suddenly, high in the canopies, a deafening chant followed them—growing louder with each call.

Blong fought his way passed PaNou to take the lead.

"Mom, what's that!"

"Now is not a good time for questions." Youa pushed PaNou from behind. "Hurry up."

"I want to be in front!" PaNou demanded.

"I'm the one who knows the way back home."

"I'm not stupid, Dad. Just follow the trail, and it'll take us straight home."

Blong ignored his daughter and marched ahead. The terrifying voice echoed louder. Their pace, hastened.

"Dad!"

No answer.

PaNou hated being ignored.

"Don't talk." Youa looked down, and shot the last bullet into the trees. BAM! The chanting stopped. While her eyes glowered, she whispered, "Pee Nyu Wai."

PaNou's face turned ghostly white. PaNou knew the stories and name too well. Pee Nyu Wai. The stories her mom used to tell resurfaced. Pee Nyu Wai: It was a hideous primate monster that fed on people, particularly children and lovers who liked to make promises—for when promises were made, a Pee Nyu Wai was listening nearby. Its chants were said to draw the human soul to it because it would devour the soul before the flesh. Although she didn't believe in such myths, PaNou's curiosity found her eyes wandering into the shadowy treetops.

Youa slapped PaNou on the shoulder, and warned, "Are you stupid! Don't you know that if you make eye contact with a Pee Nyu Wai, something really horrible will happen to you?"

Immediately, PaNou covered her face and shed tears. She was so shaken she began hopping.

"Oh, a bunch of kids you two are. Stop scaring your daughter. Are you going to pay the Shaman to call her spirit back? Your father is right here. There's no need to be afraid." As soon as Blong finished speaking, he paced faster.

"I'm not trying to scare her. Remember what happened to little Shai?"

"Shai was a dumb kid anyway. She must've ate something poisonous—"

As if in response to their conversation, the chant emerged again. This time it was directly above PaNou. PaNou's walk shifted into a track meet. Youa held the basket behind her as firm as possible and darted. They all ran with Blong scrambling to keep the lead.

Finally, Cheng got up and followed suit. His stalking ability diminished as he was simply trying not to lose the visitors. The deep chants resonated into his bones and stole his attention momentarily. The sound pulled his shoulders like two strong hands. He stopped to examine the dark ceiling. Cheng scanned the hanging branches with curiosity

42

and wanted to decipher what creature could make such a soul-devouring sound. Then branches fluttered and a few leaves fell into his hand. A figure motioned and lurked in the shadows above. A slight hissing sound echoed behind each cry. From the blackness of the treetops, two dim green dots appeared. It took a few seconds for Cheng's eyes to adjust. They grew larger by the second and then blurred like out-of-focus camera lens.

"Hurry up!" Blong yelled. His voice alarmed Cheng back to his purpose.

Cheng looked up once more. Green dots. Darkness. Green dots. Not wanting to lose them, Cheng shifted into full gear and sprinted away.

After what felt like forever, Blong, Youa, and PaNou finally reached Lou Sai. Houses crowded alongside the sandy road where a group of children congregated. Some kids were shouting. Others were crying. All were under a cloud of stench, which was from baby poop and vomit. PaNou and her parents walked through the kids without flinching. Cheng, however, tiptoed around the chaotic children, cupping his nose. When he passed them, he vacuumed any possible odor in his nose canals and spat out a large ooze of spit.

Where are their parents anyway? Cheng wondered. He looked around and caught two tiny ladies conversing at the center of the children. The elderly ladies were smaller than some of the kids. The children ran around while the countless chicks hustled left and right like tiny tennis balls. No one appeared to pay any attention to either the erratic kids or chickens.

Lou Sai was a much wealthier village than Dae Lia as demonstrated by the quality and positioning of houses. The structures had straighter roofs and walls, and they all faced the dirt roads.

Cheng found himself walking right into a festival. Booths lined the road. Some sold dried roots and herbs as medicine. Others sold tapestry blankets spread across the ground. Lou Sai was displaying a variety of food, beads, and herbs. The displays of abundant food were a scene from Cheng's dream—and no one was rushing to them. Though it was late in the evening, people were still busying themselves in chatter.

Cheng's hunger took over his purpose. For all he knew, if he lived there the fruits, papaya salads, sticky rice, and other dishes would be gone instantly. When he saw a few folks helping themselves across the other side to a steaming chicken leg, Cheng straightened his back and felt his caved belly.

Nearby, Blong's loud baritone voice once again reminded Cheng of his purpose. After nearly losing sight of them, he rushed into the multitude—now keeping a closer distance. Fortunately, for Cheng, he blended in with the visitors and the locals. Many of whom wore similar black pants, a colored sash, and either a dark vest or shirt.

Blong and Youa stopped again, laughing and speaking with a couple their own age. Then, as if PaNou sensed being followed, she turned, looking toward the booths while she fondled her hair. Cheng could easily identify her face— for PaNou stood out from the crowd like a rose in a field of dandelions. Afraid she might catch him, Cheng hopped in stride with a nearby group of men. Then steaming chicken legs and sausages caught his nose. The aroma of fresh fried food on the open table forced the deprived Cheng to dash to the booth. With exception to the scent of love, fried chicken with fish sauce and pepper had no rival.

Cheng ran his hands above the multiple plates, looking for the biggest and juiciest meat. His tongue swirled from one side to the other. Cheng failed to notice a burly woman with a pit bull-face guarding behind the table. She smiled wider than her chunky cheeks permitted. The woman kept her eyes on the new jumpy customer. The woman gleefully smiled, and held out an open hand.

"Hello." Cheng grabbed her thick hand—shaking it. "Thank you for the food." The gracious Cheng yanked a foot-long pork sausage and began vacuuming it down his throat.

The big woman stared at her empty palm. Her little brows cocked. The woman lifted the side of her mouth, revealing tainted canines. Her glittery yellow, blue, and red headscarf made her look like a terrorizing clown found only in nightmares. In the meantime, Cheng had joyfully walked away. Then he looked to where PaNou and her parents had been, but they were not in sight. Frantic, he began turning circles, oblivious that the woman with the bright scarf was barking at him.

"Hey, Kid! Get back here!"

A young man next to him tapped Cheng's shoulder. "Uh, I think you should pay for that."

Cheng looked back at the woman—her arms flailing after him. He nearly choked on the remaining rice and coughed. *What! I thought this was a sample.* At that same moment, he caught the long and flirtatious hair of PaNou waving in the distance.

"You better pay me, you little maggot!" Yelled the pit bull-faced woman. "Oh, you better not run!"

Cheng ran.

"Sorry!" Cheng regurgitated, grabbed the hand of the nearest guy, and dropped him the bits of sausage remains.

Cheng dashed toward PaNou and vowed not to lose sight of her ever again.

PaNou and her parents took an isolated path north from the main road. Along the sides to the entrance to their house grew massive banana trees, which bent inward exposing golden stalks of bananas. There were no houses behind it. The land flattened out for half a mile. The other half elevated to rolling hills that ultimately forged a series of towering jade mountains. As Cheng drew closer, the picking of bananas tempted him. He shook his head vigorously to stay focused.

The Lees' house was the largest house in Lou Sai. The structure comprised of five square sections with four units attached neatly together to a central square house. The foundation and walls were solidly built with wood and bamboo shingles. Dried elephant grass and palm leaves made the thatched roof. Unlike most houses, the Lees' was built with virtually no gaps—a symbol of their wealth.

A lush bamboo forest semicircled the property. Bright flaming poppies bloomed around the base of the house. Their petals and leaves moved like ocean waves against the wind.

Cheng brushed his front hair to one side—then dropped behind tall bushes. Through the tall blades of grass, he smiled and celebrated with each crawl as he neared the house.

Several yards from the house a bamboo fence stretched toward the mountains, encircling a dozen cows and at a least two dozen plump pigs that slumbered in the shade like giant pumpkins. The enclosed land was mostly tumbles of dirt and rocks along with patches of dying grass.

For the famished young man, the pigs were no different than dinner walking on four sticks. He missed his dad's cooking: fried pork ribs with fish sauce and pepper. That was the best! Cheng quickly grew fond of the symphony of grunts, chirps, and the mooing.

Crouching behind the bamboo clumps, he rolled out and hid behind tall shrubs, and drew closer to the house. His heart raced. Suddenly, a group of young men walked out from the house. Full of chatter, they laughed and drank heartily. Their conversation was long—too long for Cheng as he froze midway in his crawling. His left elbow and knee began to ache because most of his weight was on that side. He waited motionless until finally, the men departed. It was getting dark; the crickets had begun their ensemble and the half moon had already turned on its light. Remembering the long walk through the jungle, he breathed in his efforts and excitedly told himself he would return first thing the next day. Cheng retraced his steps behind the shrubs to the bamboo forest and back on the road.

Cheng faced the house with a longing desirous stare.

"Hello," said a man who was a few years older than Cheng. "There's a very pretty girl in there, but her dad will kill you if he catches you."

Composed, Cheng responded, "But I saw some men walking out—"

"They have to be cousins or relatives. Lucky them. I'd be her cousin a hundred times over just to talk to her." The man patted Cheng's shoulder. "Listen, there are many women out there. It's not worth it."

Cheng turned to the stranger, but the stranger left as quickly as he appeared.

Looking to the ground and at his dirt-encrusted toes, he frowned. Then Cheng stared at his right flip-flop sandal— the one with a broken blue strap, in which he had to squeeze the branch of the thong between his big and second toe every time he took a step. It was a technique he mastered, even during running. Cheng looked over to the massive house. Empty but hoping.

Cheng raced home. His heart hummed so much excitement he drop his right sandal twice. For a poor young man who had absolutely no friends, especially no money, finding where this angel lived was no different than discovering a bucket of silver bars at the end of a winding trail. He glowed with ecstasy. Somehow, someway, Cheng had to find a way to be with her.

He awoke the next day to the sun's rays beaming through the cracks of the wall. *Was it all a dream?* He rubbed his forehead. He pinched his nose with his long fingernails. There was pain. Her face—he remembered every detail. *Was she real?* He forced himself back to sleep— praying all this was not part of his imagination for there were many times before when Cheng had mistaken his dreams for reality. On one instance and a serious one, it nearly cost his life. It happened when Cheng dreamt he had found a stash of money in the ground behind a neighbor's house. When he woke up he grabbed a hoe and ran over to the fifth house to the right of his, and immediately began digging. He dug and dug until the father of the house heard him and came out. The man, short but fierce, chased him into the forest with a butcher knife. After being caught, Cheng was beaten to a twig and fined two silver bars. Because Cheng didn't have any money he ended up having to carry water and wash dishes for the man's family for a month. And for a month later, he was so sore he could barely walk.

Cheng clamped his hands together, and with eyes closed, he prayed. Next, he searched under clothes and boards for an incense stick. He found one that had an inch of life left but a match was needed. Cheng's father had often burnt an incense stick after saying a prayer to the ancestors for assistance. *No, it can't be a dream!* Then he saw something. Cheng jumped to the door and dropped on all fours. He placed his head as close to the floor as possible and studied the footprints. There they were! The different tracks of the visitors were still present. Cheng jumped to the sky, shaking his fist.

A heavy pounding on the door interrupted the moment. It opened without Cheng's response.

"Get your lazy self out to the farm. Your mom—"

"She's not my mom."

"I don't care. She paid me to keep an eye on you, Little Rat," said the bitter man who wore a large round hat. The sun drew his shadow inside.

Cheng took a heavy breath and looked at the ground.

"The farm has been infested with weeds all over. You better get your butt out there right now!"

Cheng hesitated until he thought of PaNou, and cheered, "Yes, I will go now!" He swung the basket of farm tools on to his back.

"What are you so excited about?"

"To go to the farm!" Cheng shouted.

The dour man adjusted his hat and watched as Cheng disappeared behind the houses.

The farm sat on a hillside. The land was divided into equal lots for all the villagers. A few clumps of banana trees scattered across the field. On the farm, many minded their own business. There was an occasional "Hi, how are you?" then it was straight to work: tend the crops, pull the weeds, and the worst part, water the plants. The nearest creek was at least a few hundred yards away. After a few trips, the distance felt twice as long and the water bucket felt many times heavier.

It had always felt hotter on the farm. Despite the abundance of weeds, Cheng's prior labor was finally showing results. The sugarcanes were taller than Cheng, and in two weeks the watermelons, cucumbers, and tomatoes would be ripe for picking.

Rather than working on the farm, on this particular day he hid his basket of sickle, hoe, and pail under a bush. With the wind behind him, Cheng flew with endless energy to Lou Sai. He lost his right sandal but quickly recovered it and ran again—chest out in front.

Like a scholar, Cheng spent two days observing—calculating his next big move. To be near her presence was worth it! Simply watching PaNou making her way in and out of the house was exhilarating. He studied her family, their patterns, and their house. Cheng soon gathered that the Lees received numerous visitors—that her mom was up half an hour before the rooster's crow to tend the farm, and that her father smoked opium in a massive bamboo pipe twice a day—once, when the sun rose against the mountains, and second, when the sun rested into the reddening sky before a line of women returned from the fields. Finally, he gathered the most important treasure: the location of PaNou's room. Her room was adjacent to the thickest set of shrubs—facing the mountains. It was also on the opposite end of her parents' room. Perfect!

On the third day, Cheng could no longer hold his anxiety. When PaNou's parents left the house, he pounced on the opportunity. Once again, his hunting ability proved useful. Like a panther, he crept behind every bush, tree, and shadow without making a sound. Finally, he reached the blossoming poppies. There, he snaked his way to her room, and sat pressed against the wall. Digging his shirt pocket, he pulled out a *ncas*, a tiny mouth harp made from brass. It glimmered back as if to say, "What are you waiting for, Dummy? Now is the time to play me!"

Cheng stared blankly at the wall—inhaled deeply, rolled up his sleeves, and circled his shoulders. He kissed his knuckles before giving a few soft knocks. Heart pounding, he pressed the ncas to the front of his lips, and with the thumb of the other hand, he strummed the end. Gentle streams of air ignited from his lungs, followed by the warmth of his heart. Lips set free. Eyes closed—a soothing, robotic sound shuffled through the wall to initiate conversation. Eyes opened. Its rhythmic buzzing tamed his racing heart. So captivating was the reverberation even the pushy wind halted and the pigs ceased their snorting; all life yielded to the playing of the tiny mouth harp.

From inside, a body leaned against the wall. "Who's there?" asked a sweet but demanding voice. Her tone was rapid and somewhat irritated.

Cheng leaned his head against the wall and sat straighter. With more confidence, he choked out his first word, "Hi." Cheng didn't want to speak too loudly, as he didn't want to sound rude but there was no answer. Again, he persisted with a few knocks, "Hello. My name's Cheng."

"Stop it with your stupid jokes, Fong. You monkey! I'm not that stupid."

She already has a boyfriend! Cheng slumped in devastated silence.

"Fong," she called.

No answer.

"Fong!"

Fong? The thought of another man courting her nearly stopped his heart.

The silence that followed passed like eternity.

There was no response except the sound of her shuffling about behind the windowless wall. Cheng gripped the ncas to his chest, and with dread, he lowered it. He rose, and with the ncas inside his fist, Cheng punched at the sky, at life. Life wasn't fair to him—never had been.

"Hey, you're not Fong," PaNou said, shocked.

Cheng nearly fell while turning around. His eyes shot swiftly at her face then down to her slender legs and back to her stunning eyes, hoping she didn't catch him doing that. It was unmistakably her—the candy-green sandals, the dark-arch brows, and the long jet-black hair flowing like a cape behind her shoulders.

"You, have we met?" Her bold voice overcame him. PaNou looked into the azure sky, scanning her memory.

In the pause, Cheng's eyes scanned her brilliant features. Like a pressured pipe about to explode, Cheng squeezed his eyes shut, and mumbled, "Uh." For all he could think of were two things: how beautiful she was and Fong, the lucky guy who beat him to her.

Puzzled, PaNou pondered with an essence of allure, meanwhile Cheng couldn't stop gazing at her black pearl eyes whirling in circles.

"Gosh, where have I seen you?" PaNou asked, tapping her chin—oblivious of Cheng's dying affection.

"Who's Fong?" Cheng questioned with the maximum exertion of his lungs.

She didn't answer—still wondering where she had seen him.

Drowned in desperation, he tightened the front ends of his mucky red sash. *How stupid could I be? A beautiful girl like this—if she isn't married, she has a man,* Cheng thought. Though prepared for the worst, Cheng had to know who this "Fong" was.

Her luscious lips stretched to the left, in an unintentionally seductive manner.

Cheng held his breath.

"Oh, yeah!" she proclaimed.

Eyes widened, Cheng could feel every ounce of his life flushing away. Her sudden excitement made him slouch lower—uncertain if it was because Fong's name was mentioned or a miracle happened and she remembered him. In anticipation, Cheng began chewing his bottom lip.

PaNou held out her index finger as she spoke, "Oh, right! Gosh, we were supposed to go to Choua's house, but we went to your house instead. If I remember correctly, I don't think we even knocked, did we?" A bit embarrassed, she continued, "Sorry. My dad, he never asks for directions. He thinks he knows everything."

"Hey, no problem," Cheng said. "We're all Hmong, so you're always welcome." Discretely, he stood higher on his toes, as he realized her taller eyes were looking down at him. Peaking at almost five and a half foot short, with long scrappy hair, bushy eyebrows, and one set of clothing, Cheng was the anti-Prince Charming.

"How did you find out where I live?"

"Well," Cheng's eyes rolled away, "we're all Hmong. Everybody knows everybody." His brain was about to burst, praying for her to stop investigating. *What would she think of me if she found out? A stalker, a pervert!*

PaNou returned Cheng an unusual look. Then smiled, "Yeah, that's one thing I hate about being Hmong. When you do something good, everyone knows, and when you do something bad, everyone knows too."

Cheng nodded in complete agreement meanwhile his mind still couldn't let go of the mysterious Fong. Scratching his chin frivolously, Cheng said, "So, uh, this Fong guy. He must be really handsome and tall. I'm sure he's rich too."

"Oh gosh, he's rich all right. Rich in stupidity," PaNou laughed.

"Oh," Cheng frowned with confusion, but more importantly, a sense of relief.

"Fong," she said, "is my younger brother, and he always, I mean he's *always* coming up with the dumbest ways to scare me." Her eyes enlarged and then she broke into another round of laughter, "And you know what? The only thing he scares is himself!"

Cheng forcefully jolted out a laugh to collaborate with hers. "I'd like to meet him—"

"No you don't. You might regret it," PaNou said, shaking her head. Her eyebrows folded inward in seriousness, unaware that she had injected an enchanted joy into the young man.

"It'd be *great* to meet him."

"No, seriously, you don't want to meet him." She slid her hair behind her right ear.

"Just curious," Cheng said, scratching the back of his head, "what did your parents feed you?"

PaNou looked confused initially, and thought, *Am I that fat?* She looked at Cheng's sly smile and then quickly discerned his humor about her height and beauty. She simply laughed, and held out three fingers. "Rice for breakfast, rice for lunch, rice for dinner."

"And for snacks."

"Yes!" PaNou slightly tilted her head down. Then she rolled her eyes up with an open smile.

"And what do your parents call you?"

"PaNou."

"Pa...Nou." He breathed her name. "That's a beautiful name. And your last name?"

Cheng prayed she wasn't a Yang like he was, especially when Yang was the largest clan of the Hmong—for it was considered the same as marrying a sister despite no direct relation.

Cheng's eyelids curled back, holding his breath.

"Lee. And you?" She was growing fond of the awkward young man. His dark hair and oversized sad-looking brown eyes gave him an innocent, yet playful demeanor.

"A Lee..." Cheng, who was in his own world echoed her words and had to maintain his excitement.

"You're a Lee, too?" PaNou curled her lips.

"No. No," Cheng said, tossing his arms in defense. "I was just repeating what you said. My last name is Yang. Cheng Yang." Cheng nodded and gave a reassuring smile.

She, too, smiled back.

"PaNou! PaNou!" scolded a woman from inside the house. "Where'd you put my shirt?"

Cheng began to panic and his left knee jerked like he was in a trance—one leg desperately wanting to detach and take off while the other was planted solid. PaNou watched, amused.

"That's my mom," whispered PaNou, chuckling at Cheng's quivering.

Cheng blushed.

"PaNou! Where is that lazy girl?"

PaNou tilted her head in annoyance.

Cheng begged with his eyes for her to do something to extend their moment. PaNou's lips widened, and she faced the house.

"Mom! It's in Dad's room."

"What?"

"It's in Dad's room! Like always!"

"What are you doing outside?"

"I-I was just over to feed the chickens."

Cheng's small body shrunk even smaller. Then she brought her index finger up and pressed it against her squeezed lips.

"Shhh…"

Cheng's face switched instantaneously from chalk white to tomato red. His expression and color changed so fast PaNou couldn't hold her quietness and cried in laughter.

"What's so funny?—"

"Nothing, Mom. It was a pig falling over itself."

Youa chuckled.

By now the scorching sun had climbed dead center. Most of the farm animals had congregated under a few trees. The clapping of sandals grew louder from the house.

"Your father will be home soon. Let me come out and help you so we can start making lunch."

"It's okay, Mom. I finished it. Why don't you start making lunch and I'll help you in a bit?"

"I should be going now," Cheng whispered, nervously. "Uh, can I see you tomorrow?"

"Sure." PaNou lifted her shoulders. "I'll be here. I'm not allowed to go anywhere, anyway." PaNou tucked her hair behind her ear.

"Four knocks."

"What?"

Cheng smiled and gave four knocks on his palm.

She smiled, and nodded.

"See you tomorrow then." Like a ninja, Cheng ducked low and hurried into the nearby forest.

PaNou watched until he disappeared. *He's a bit weird, but funny.*

Cheng walked home, electrified with happiness—tomorrow afternoon couldn't come fast enough. PaNou was also very excited, for her life was uneventful; everyday consisted of cooking, cleaning, massaging her parents, and sometimes doing needlework and learning traditional songs. The most exciting moment was laundry—at least then she was outside and could play in the small river where she washed. Cheng was a fresh breath of life and PaNou looked forward to seeing his delightful presence again.

Four weeks passed. Cheng visited PaNou without missing a day. They conversed, smiled, shared stories, and Cheng said a few stupid things on occasion that made PaNou laugh. His charismatic and consistent efforts won the young woman's heart. Before PaNou had realized, she had fallen in love with him as much as with his stories about loss, hunger, and integrity.

"How do you know so many stories?"

"My father, he used to tell me stories all the time."

"Can you tell me another one?"

"Sure." Cheng took some time to think of one that she might really like. "Let's see...have you heard the story about Tou Cha and the Dragon?"

"No, I don't think so. Is it a scary story?"

"No."

"Okay," she sat straighter from behind the wall. "Go on."

"Okay. Tou Cha, he was an orphan boy, like me I guess."

"Don't say that. You have your father."

"Some days, anyway, Tou Cha's parents died when he was about four years old. So he went to live with his grandmother who loved him very much. But a few years later when his grandmother remarried, her new husband didn't want Tou Cha, so they kicked him out. So *then* Tou Cha had no place to live."

"How could they be so mean?"

"Well, he got by with food by doing side jobs and chores around the village. Then one day when he got older, he saw this one girl. Her name was Mai Kou, and she was, oh—the most beautiful thing he'd ever seen." For the moment, Cheng pictured PaNou's smile and continued, "But you see, her family was super wealthy, and Tou Cha, well, he was an orphan." Cheng paused, realizing just how similar the story was to his present situation.

"Yeah, and what happened?"

"Okay, Mai Kou really liked Tou Cha too, but everyone hated him because he didn't have anything. Well, her parents found out they were seeing each other, and one day while Mai Kou's father was making fun of Tou Cha, and I mean in front of everyone, he made a joke and gave his word to all of the people there that if Tou Cha could ever come up with twenty silver bars in a month, he would allow Tou Cha to marry his daughter, *and* also receive the family's entire property. Oh, and also Mai Kou's father would eat cow poop for everyone to watch."

"That's a *big* promise."

"Yeah, but it was impossible for Tou Cha to get half that much money in his lifetime," Cheng said. "Well, it got worse for the orphan boy. Because afterward, when he worked, people no longer paid him. Then people stopped giving him work. He became very, *very* sad. He went to his father's grave and he cried all through the night.

"Then one day there was a group of men that finally offered to pay him for sweeping around the house. Tou Cha was so happy he went back to his father's grave to say thanks. By then, he had only two or three weeks left to come up with the rest of the money, which again was impossible. Well, after the three men paid him, they followed him to a nearby lake, beat him up, took the money, and tossed him into the green lake."

"Oh, my gosh."

"You see, this green lake was very deep. So deep, it had a magical red dragon that guarded the water and fish. It was said that there was a man who saw the dragon and became blind a year later. Anyway, Tou Cha couldn't swim. So, when the men didn't see him come out, they got scared and took off. Three days passed and there was no sight of him. On the following night, some villagers claimed they heard loud splashes in the water. Soon, the villagers spread rumors that Tou Cha was swallowed by the Lake Dragon—"

"He was inside the dragon's belly."

"You've heard of this story before?" Cheng sounded disappointed because he wanted to tell her the rest.

"No, I haven't. I was just guessing, I mean—"

Cheng smiled, "He was. Tou Cha was inside the dragon's belly, and there, he found tons of treasure. There were so many gold coins, he was swimming in them! But after three days of no food, Tou Cha thought he was going to die. He knew no one was coming to look for him, so with every passing night he prayed and prayed to the sky. Then on the fifth night, he found a sword plated with diamonds and pearls. With the sword, Tou Cha cut the dragon's belly and escaped with his pockets full of treasures. Finally, on the sixth day he walked to Mai Kou's house, and the person who opened the door was—"

"Mai Kou!"

"No. Mai Kou's dad."

PaNou began laughing.

"Yep, Tou Cha poured all the coins from his sash as if it were raining gold. He had many times over twenty silver bars—"

"He got to be with Mai Kou!" PaNou said.

Cheng thought it was rude for her to keep interrupting him but continued, "Yes, he did. Tou Cha gave the rest of the gold away because his real treasure was Mai Kou. They got married, got the property, and he also kept the sword."

"That's a really sweet story." PaNou stared joyfully at the ceiling.

"Thanks. Could you imagine the look on her father's face? Well, the people didn't forget the promise made by Mai Kou's father. So yeah, he had to eat cow poop in front of the entire village."

The both of them laughed.

"Oh, shhh," PaNou reminded. She couldn't remember a time when she was this excited and had to quiet herself from laughing. Sure, Cheng wasn't the most handsome guy she had come across, but he was certainly fun and also had an awkward sincerity.

Since they met, Cheng's visits had been full of jubilant conversations until a few nights later when the tone of their magical conversation took a shift.

"Cheng, I'm glad you came. I heard...I heard what happened." She rocked her head against the wall. "It's my fault. I forgot to tell you." PaNou spoke from inside the wall.

"Can you talk a bit louder? I can't hear you." Cheng clamped his ear to the wall.

"Two days ago, I overheard my dad talking to some men, telling them to—"

"Oh, yeah." Cheng's voice shook with thick pain.

PaNou sensed agony in his voice. Her heart grew heavy.

"This morning, some punks snuck behind my house, waited until I came out, then they attacked me."

PaNou gripped her face.

"If it was one-on-one, I could've beaten them." Cheng paused, and after taking a breath he continued, "This one guy with long hair hammered me with this really *fat* stick. Thank goodness, it broke after a couple hits. Otherwise, I don't think they would've ever stopped. I really thought I was going to die. My whole life flashed by."

"I'm, I'm so sorry. I wanted to tell you, but I forgot." PaNou folded her face in frustration. "Maybe..." She drew out a long breath. "Maybe you shouldn't come here anymore."

"Why? There's someone else, isn't there?"

"No, Cheng. There's no one else." She placed her chin on her hand. "I'm just saying maybe we should take a break."

"Why are you saying that?"

"I can't, Cheng. I can't bear anyone hurting you."

"PaNou, until the day you tell me there's another man in your heart, I'll be here no matter what. Even if your dad brings a thousand men to beat me, I'll still visit you."

"To be honest, Cheng, and don't take this the wrong way, but when I met you, I never thought I-I was going to care so much about you. But I—never mind. It's silly."

"No. Tell me."

"It's because every time someone hurts you, it hurts me too."

"Don't worry about me. I'm fine now. Talking with you is already making me feel better," said Cheng. "I don't understand why your dad hates me so much."

"I don't understand him either. What I do know is when my dad's angry, he can kill someone. He has a short temper. Out of all my siblings, I'm the only one that stands up to him and *that* really angers him."

"I think people like *him* should be the ones going to war." Cheng grinned, proud of his own clever advice.

"Yes, you're so right. He did try, but I think they kicked him out because he was too fat." She paused. "Cheng, I'm lucky to have someone like you."

59

"You're just saying that."

"I mean it. First time I've said that to anyone."

"Well, first time anyone has said that to me." Cheng stared at the wall with eyes closed, imagining he was looking at PaNou. "I'm the luckiest guy on earth."

"Something is happening to me that I've never imagined, and I like it."

"PaNou! Who are you talking to?" Youa's footsteps drew near.

PaNou rapidly whispered, "I have to go."

"See you tomorrow," said Cheng, and he hurried away.

"PaNou!" Youa marched into her room. "Are you deaf? Why are you not answering?"

"I talk to myself, Mom. That's what I do when I'm stressed."

"Stressed? What could you be stressed about? You have your mom and dad. We take care of everything here for you. All you do is eat and poop."

"I need time alone, okay."

"You and your father! I can't understand you two. If other people hear you talking to yourself they might think you've lost your mind." She grabbed the front panel of her garment and pulled it straight. Then she turned her eyes back to PaNou. "Get up! We have visitors coming. Wipe the table and sweep the floor."

"It's so late, why are people still coming—"

"Get up, right now."

"I'll be there."

"Now means NOW!"

PaNou never hated doing chores as much as at that moment. She was already looking forward to tomorrow. To Cheng.

At noon each day, Cheng's routine consisted of sneaking past the bamboo forest, rolling through the tall grass, snaking behind clumps of thick bushes, and finally waiting outside

PaNou's room. Exhausted indeed but very much worth the effort. There, he played his ncas—and captivated her.

"PaNou, hearing your voice washes away all my worries."

"You really know how to put it into words because that's how I feel listening to your music," said PaNou, eyes shut and heart wide open.

"This piece is for you." Cheng strummed the ncas and it spoke:

My Sweetheart, can it be true that you are mine?
If I could buy anything, I'd buy you all the stars,
To show you how much I need you in my life,
I want to caress your sweet laughter in my arms,
To keepsake for all eternity.
Like the sun and flower,
I belong to you and you to me.
My love will pour your way like an endless shower,
For I know nothing but to love you for eternity.

The tiny harp's soft buzzing voice mesmerized her. Pressing her head against the wall, and with her knees bent to her chest, she smiled, "Cheng, your ncas plays right into my heart."

Cheng was folded in the same position outside.

She hummed, running her fingers through her hair. "How do you play so well?"

"My song is only as beautiful as the person I'm playing for."

She blushed. "I'm sure you say that to every girl you meet."

"No, I'm serious," Cheng defended. "Besides, how could you say 'every girl I meet'? You're the first one...and in my heart, the last." He turned to face the wall. "You know I'll always be here for you. PaNou, please know you're the only one I love and I hope you won't get tired of me."

There was silence from her. Without seeing her expression, Cheng feared he might have sounded too desperate. He resented.

"You probably are sick of me now," Cheng broke the quietness.

"No. It's not that."

Holding the ncas in front of him by the string, he swung it back and forth like a pendulum. "Sometimes I really wonder how a beautiful girl like you is without a boyfriend."

Although Cheng couldn't see her, PaNou's cheeks reddened like cherries.

"Well, you should thank my parents. They rarely let me out."

"Still, there must've been guys—"

"Well, you should know why. It's because of my dad. Many would never dare visit me. Those that did, my dad scared all of them away."

"Yes, I can believe that." Cheng felt the bruises on his shoulder.

"Um, there was this *one* guy. His name was Doua." She paused, remembering him. "Light skinned. The only guy my parents and I ever liked. Very tall and handsome. Deep voice. He had these nice big arms."

"Really?" Cheng deepened his voice. Hurt. Uninterested but respectful. "So what happened?" He began feeling the size of his wimpy biceps.

"He was a Lee."

"Sorry to hear that." Cheng wasn't. Rather relieved. "Were you two related at all?"

"I don't know. My parents didn't know his family. At the time, I didn't care because I liked him. They were just passing by from a far village and needed a place to rest."

"At the beginning of human life, we all came from the same mom and dad."

PaNou laughed. "You're right. If you think about it, it's all disgusting."

Cheng lifted his chest. "So how come you're with me? Maybe you're playing with my heart."

"You need to stop saying those things."

"Seriously, why are you with me?"

"...well, you're different. You have guts."

"I do?" Cheng questioned, unsure of how attractive having guts was. "I mean thanks." He grinned.

"And you're awkward."

Awkward looking? Cheng prayed not.

PaNou stared into space and continued, "Gosh, it's so dead boring here..."

Boring? Cheng hoped it wasn't because of him.

"Every day, I have to stay in the house or in the back-yard. You're probably the best thing that's happened to me. At least I have someone who understands me."

"Why don't your parents let you out?"

"They don't want me playing with boys unless they're relatives. Since I was a kid, I was told my belly would swell up if I talk to boys. I believed it so much I wished all boys were dead."

"Whoa, you took it seriously."

"Well, of course. When I was a kid, I believed every-thing my parents said." Leaning against the wall, she switched from her back to her side.

"And now?"

"Hey, I do grow up too," PaNou said. A tint of hap-piness sung from her voice. "There are guys. Then there's you." With her finger, she began drawing Cheng's figure on the wall. "You're short, scrawny, and you never change your shirt."

Cheng frowned—his heart began to collapse in pro-test. *So what if this happens to be my only shirt. It's my favorite shirt!* He grabbed the collar, and began studying it.

"But really, you're a good person," continued PaNou. "Honest with a big heart."

Even after weeks of visiting her daily, Cheng still doubted PaNou's feelings for him. Her beauty was his insecurity. And he wanted continued assurance but didn't want to portray himself as desperate.

"How could you tell?" Cheng rolled up his sleeves—relieved she still had good opinions of him.

"You wouldn't know how to be bad if you tried." PaNou laughed, "Goofball."

"Yeah, well, you're a...uh..." Cheng paused. He liked her too much—too much to dare say anything bad.

"See what I mean."

"Sure. Pretty funny. Well, I do hope to be good enough to earn your love one day," Cheng said softly—hoping for her to answer his plea immediately.

She didn't. There was silence behind the wall. Cheng only wished he could see her expression. Then he could tell how she felt.

Cheng weighed his shoulder against the wall. Waiting for her to say those magical words he had diligently worked so hard for. After all, he'd told her, "I love you," a few times already. Instead, she sat and remained quiet. "I don't really know how to say this." Cheng took a deep breath, and PaNou could feel his nervousness vibrating through the wall.

"Yes?" PaNou asked, thinking he might ask her something crazy, like marry him.

Cheng spoke slowly, emphasizing each word. "Will you give me permission to love you?"

The question caught her off-guard. Chin tucked, thoughts cluttered her mind for a brief moment—unsure how to react. It was like asking her to marry him, but then, it wasn't. Nonetheless, she looked to the ceiling. Heart softened, she smiled. "Yes," PaNou responded with mostly breath.

It took a few seconds before the single word sank in. Cheng felt like jumping and screaming at the top of his lungs. Instead, he displayed his usual nerdy manner.

"Thanks."

She raised an eyebrow. "You're welcome." And giggled, liking Cheng's etiquette.

"I promise to love you with all my heart." Cheng searched for those magical words.

"I am very lucky."

Cheng smiled, and nodded. "No, I'm the lucky one."

The following four days brought a thunderous rainfall that poured relentlessly. Each day pelted down more powerful rain. Despite the heavy rain, Cheng showed up, drenched, but full of vigor.

On the fourth day, the rain drummed the roof so loud that they couldn't hear their conversation. So when Cheng began raising his voice, PaNou snuck outside. She crept behind the still chatting Cheng, and from behind, she cupped her hand over his mouth—nearly scaring the life out of him.

"Shhh." She gently pulled his face around.

Eyelids yanked back, Cheng obliged.

"Don't talk so loud. You don't want to wake up my dad." Her face possessed a subtle glow under the wet and gloomy weather.

A thunder erupted, followed by an echo across the mountains. Cheng found higher ground so they could be at the same eye level.

"Why are you staring at me like that?" Her eyes followed his.

"Your cheeks—they're naturally pink and beautiful."

"Thanks. I haven't said this to you, but I like your eyes a lot. They're really big. I think they're pretty."

Pretty? Cheng didn't know what to make of such a remark and stood there, studying her features.

"Now stop staring at me like that."

"Sorry, sometimes I can't help it. Your lips. They are as red as the poppies and your hair—"

"Oh, stop that! You're being silly." That was the last comment she'd expect out in the torrential rainfall. The heavy raindrops pounded their heads and clothing. She gazed at the black clouds and waved both her arms. "Hey stop. You can stop anytime now."

"It's like standing under a waterfall. It hasn't rained this much since I was a small boy." Cheng cupped his hand to catch the large raindrops, and it overflowed in seconds. "Heck, when it rained this much I used to dig a large hole in the ground and pretended I was sailing across this *grand* ocean." Cheng extended his arms to draw out the ocean.

PaNou's eyes widened and so did her smile.

"Yeah! Then, I'd grab small sticks and imagine they were these giant ships and—"

"Let's make one!" She quickly tied her long hair.

"Now?"

He wasn't sure if PaNou meant it or not. Too late. PaNou was already digging into the mud while bullets of rain continued to unleash.

"Hey, stop laughing! What's so funny?" asked PaNou as she continued digging with her fingertips.

"It'll take you a hundred years if you dig like that."

PaNou ignored him and increased her pace.

"All right, let me show you."

He knelt beside her. With his entire hands and forearms buried into the mud, Cheng began shoveling out buckets of dirt. Shortly after, the two had created a crater half a foot deep with a circumference of a small dining table. Cheng stood up and scanned their environment.

"What're you looking for?" asked PaNou.

"We need rocks."

"Rocks? For what?"

"Watch the pro."

Cheng quickly fed upon the excitement and became the small boy that he once was. He grabbed rocks alongside the house, aligning them around their ocean.

"There. This way the rain doesn't push any more dirt into it."

PaNou grinned in acknowledgement of Cheng's expertise.

"Cool, huh?"

"We need ships too. So we can travel across the great ocean." PaNou began breaking a large stick into strips. She held up a strip with a hole in it. It looked like a miniature canoe. "Okay, here's my ship."

"That's a nice one."

"And here's yours."

"Thanks!"

In a few minutes, the rain filled their "ocean."

"Yeah, now we can travel the entire world." Cheng snatched her "ship" and guided it to the opposite end. PaNou seized it back from Cheng, and suddenly stopped in motion.

"What's wrong?"

"Nothing," PaNou said. "You're crazy."

"Crazy? No, you're crazy. You started this."

"No. We're both crazy. Look at us!"

The two looked at each other. Both covered in mud. With her forearm, PaNou wiped her forehead, only to spread more mud across it.

"Don't stop now. C'mon." Cheng turned to look at the overflowing puddle. The kid inside was alive. He continued playing and splashing.

"Hey, Cheng."

Cheng looked up, a bit annoyed because she interrupted him.

Immediately, she launched a ball of spongy mud, hitting Cheng dead center on the face. It splattered into his mouth and nostrils, masking him.

"Pyyyyuck!" Cheng knelt over, spitting.

"How does it taste?"

"Like mud."

PaNou laughed.

"What was that for anyway?"

"For...thanks!" She calmed her laughter. "You're fun to be with."

"Fun to throw mud at, you mean."

"No. I'm serious now. You're fun to be with." There was a sudden change in her expression. PaNou then moved her ship across the puddle. "Let's go to France!"

"No. No. Let's go to Australia!" Cheng turned both ships to the left.

"What's Awwhstri—?" PaNou seized Cheng's wrist.

"Australia. I heard it's a land far away, across the ocean somewhere. That's why I want to go there. Come on."

"No! I want to go to France." PaNou took her ship back and placed it opposite from Cheng's.

"We should stick together," advised Cheng, who was taking the game seriously.

PaNou ignored his suggestion. "Gosh, we should do this every day."

"If we did this every day, you'd be bored with it."

"Not if you eat mud." She fired another ball of mud that splashed his left arm.

"You want war—you got it."

Jet fighter planes roared like a volcanic eruption through the low-lying clouds, shuddering the trees nearby. The dark clouds had a monstrous feel to their power. The booming sound created ripples on their ocean. Cheng shrunk low, while PaNou stood taller.

"A-4 fighter planes. Americans."

"How do you know?"

"I can tell from the sound. Did you see them? They were flying so low." Just when PaNou's eyes were tracing the vanishing sounds to the north, Cheng fired an onslaught of mud balls. One splattered behind her head.

Oops! Cheng was aiming for her shoulder.

The one that hit her head pained her a bit and she protested, "Hey! You promised to love me, so you can't throw mud at me."

"I do. I love you and I LOOOVVVVE throwing mud at you." Cheng was now the one laughing while PaNou ducked for cover. This time he threw them lower.

The two went at it, tossing and splattering mud at each other. Enjoying every bit of it.

The commotion caught Fong's attention as he walked into PaNou's room. Realizing it was from outside, he walked out to the laughter.

Nearing fifteen years of age, Fong was the tallest of all his friends—stretching five foot nine. Unlike PaNou, he had his father's nose: round, short, and stretched wider than his mouth. His dark hair covered his head like a bowl. His acne-infested face and meaty build made him look much older—until his personality took over. Fong was a prankster by nature.

Yes! She's gonna get it this time! Fong rubbed his hands as he watched. Meanwhile, PaNou and Cheng were blissful in their little world—completely unaware of Fong surveying from behind the corner of the house. The couple continued with their mud war. Hastily, Fong ran inside. Minutes later, an agitated Blong woke from his hibernation. He marched outside, followed by Fong.

A shadow emerged. Widest at center. PaNou's expression iced while still holding a fresh ball of mud. Cheng's eyes followed PaNou's, and he turned around to look up. There, less than ten yards away stood Blong—a tall man with midget legs, oversized hips, bulging belly, and a large grizzly bear nose.

"I'm sorry, we were—" Cheng said.

"Are you two humans or pigs?" Blong interrupted, crossed his arms—eyes scrutinizing the couple.

Carefully, PaNou wiped the mud from her forehead and skirt. Such effort was futile because they were completely covered with mud.

"You see those pigs there?" Blong pointed to the fence where pigs and cows cuddled in their own groups.

PaNou and Cheng looked. In the near distance, two pigs rested like giant brown pillows—snorting in their slumber.

Like a weasel, Fong popped from the house. He wrapped his hands around his mouth, holding back an explosion of laughter. It was perfect vengeance for the trip to Dae Lia.

"Both of you are dumber than those pigs," Blong swung his head. "Is that mud or cow dung that you two are covered with?"

Cheng cringed at PaNou and shamefully, turned away.

"Dad—" PaNou tucked her hands under her armpits.

"Shut your mouth, or I'll cut your tongue off and feed it to the pigs."

People could call Cheng names and he could live through it, but the way Blong was yelling at PaNou harpooned his heart. Pushing his sleeves further up, Cheng slapped his soaked hair back and straightened his back. *I have to say something. I have to.*

PaNou's father reclined his head, displaying oversized nostrils. Without moving his neck, Blong's eyeballs glared at Cheng, staring him down. Upon recognizing the young man's face and, more importantly, his rudeness from their prior encounter, Blong's eyebrows tightened.

"You're that miserable *orphan*."

"Dad, we were just having fun. Can't I live life for once?"

"I'm not an orphan. I have a father," Cheng said, though he had little respect for his own father.

"You! You *are* an orphan! Else you'd know your manners." Blong turned to his daughter. "PaNou, tell your *pig* here to get the hell out of this place. We have enough pigs already."

Cheng cleared his throat. "Sorry, but what you're saying is not right. You—" Cheng gulped his saliva.

"If your life has any value to you, then get your dirty face out of my sight!" Blong stomped closer to Cheng.

"Dad, stop it!" PaNou stepped in front of Cheng, confronting her father. "How could you say such things? We're all human beings."

The thunder of fighter planes erupted overhead, followed by intense gun firings and bomb explosions on the mountainside. Blong stood, indifferent to the bombings. In recent years such blasts became a norm to the Hmong like the dawn crowing of roosters. Then a sudden and lively exchange of artillery ricocheted throughout the high hills. Spots of orange and white illuminated the hillsides. The gunshots gave Blong an idea.

"Perhaps this pig understands a bullet better." Blong returned to the house.

"Cheng!" PaNou turned to Cheng and started pushing him. "Cheng! Get out of here. Now!"

Cheng slipped and fell, and struggled to get back up.

With eyes closed, she continued shouting. The pushing became open-hand punches.

Cheng anchored his legs and absorbed her punches—until finally PaNou's knees dropped to the ground, followed by her hands and head. She grabbed him by his shirt, and struggled to speak. Cheng looked over to the house where Blong had disappeared. His eyes reddened.

"You promised you'll love me no matter what," she wept. "So why aren't you doing what I'm telling you?"

Cheng didn't budge.

"Do you love me like you keep saying?" Shaking frantically, PaNou looked at Cheng's round eyes, switching rapidly from one to the other.

In the distance, the exchange of gunshots grew livelier.

Cheng exhaled. Long and loud. A massive explosion took their attention to the mountains. The fiery blasts brightened the dark sky like day for a brief moment. Cheng saw the reflection of the mushroom-shaped explosion from PaNou's sparkling eyes. He lifted his hand and caressed her right cheek. PaNou was cold, scared, and shivering.

PaNou pulled him nearer. "Do you truly love me?"

"I love you with all of my heart."

"Then listen to me, please? Get out of here!" she begged. Looking at the soggy ground, she scrubbed some mud from Cheng's feet and smeared it over her own toes, and said quietly, "Go...run away and don't ever come back."

"How could you say those words to me?" Tears rolled down Cheng's cheeks, but they blended with the rain.

"I-I don't know!" The frustrated PaNou snatched her hair, pulling it.

"You don't know!" Cheng echoed her words. "You don't know, huh…" He looked to the sky, at the sullen clouds.

"I…"

Cheng brushed her wet and sticky hair to the left side of her face. "I get it. You don't ever want to see me again," Cheng breathed. "I understand now. You were playing with my heart all this time. How twisted could your heart be? You could've just told me." Cheng kicked the mud. Some accidentally flew to her face. "For some time, I actually believed you, in us! Your father is right. I *am* as dumb as a pig. Look at me! I'm nobody. I'm just an *orphan* boy with one shirt." He tore his shirt apart, breaking the remaining button and tossed it to the side. Cheng wiped his soaked brows. "I have nothing to offer you…just only this." Cheng's muddy hand gripped his left chest. Then he dropped his hands to his sides. The rain pouring—washing the dirt down his chest.

PaNou dug her knees deeper into the spongy ground. Then, motionless.

"Yeah, go ahead. Kick me out like a pig. One day when you—"

"I love you." PaNou hid her face in her hands, and she began shaking.

Cheng stopped his denouncing. He dropped. Then gently he kissed her on the forehead. Those magic three words—"I love you" had poured from the deepest and most hidden caverns of her heart.

"Then why are you hitting me? Why are you yelling at me to get out of here?"

"Because my dad *really* has a gun in the house. And he's crazy enough that he'll *really* shoot you."

Cheng looked up at the corner of the house and un-expectedly took a glimpse of Fong who was watching. Fong turned away, hiding himself behind the house.

"I'm sorry—" PaNou said.

"Don't."

"You don't deserve any of this."

"Neither do you. I love you and I'm going to take us out of this place. You have my word."

Shuffling sounds came from the house. "Where did you put my rifle?" Blong's voice rumbled from inside.

"What! What in the world do you need a rifle for? Are you crazy, Old Man?"

PaNou looked back to the house. "Please, please go."

Cheng lowered his head, picked up his muddy shirt, and without a further second vanished into the murky rain.

A brief moment later, Blong returned with an M-14 strapped over his shoulder. He aimed at the tall bushes, the farm, and the dark bamboo forest. No one was in sight except PaNou who curled up and shook like an injured animal.

"Where's that pig of yours?"

PaNou did not respond.

"At least that pig knows fear."

PaNou ignored her father and continued moving the tiny sticks across the ocean she and Cheng had created.

"PaNou, are you a human or a dog? Even a dog is smart enough not to dig its own grave." Blong pointed his index finger at her. "Listen carefully. If I ever, *ever,* see you again with that orphan boy, I will slice his throat and then sue him all the way to his ancestors!"

The rain continued its downpour—pounding heavier on her face, her shoulders, her heart.

"Dad—"

"No." Blong held his rifle firmly. "Let the sky above witness that if you ever decide to go off with that orphan, your life will be condemned and both of you will suffer greatly. You listen. I gave birth to you so you must obey my every word." Blong wasted no further words and returned to the house.

Fong, who was still observing, revealed his full self from the corner. For the first time, he wasn't laughing or celebrating his victory. The moment PaNou looked up and saw Fong's face, she knew.

"Fong!" She didn't have the energy to get up and give him a beating.

"Hey, you two were making so much noise and I—" Fong coughed his words. Guilt saturated his face.

"You two! Get back in the house. Only animals could be out in this rain," said Blong as he walked past Fong. "PaNou, if you're not inside in one minute, I'm bringing the whip."

Fong raced back inside before PaNou could have more words.

On all fours, PaNou clawed to the rocks that circled their ocean. She lifted her ship and set it next to Cheng's. And like the rainstorm, her tears poured into the ocean. As if lightning had zapped her body, she fell forward into the puddle of water and punched her hands into the bottom, stopping her face an inch away from splashing into the water. Her long hair fell forward, swimming across the surface.

I wish...I wish I was never born into this life. What is there to live for?

A shadowy figure appeared in front of her. Though she felt someone coming closer, she remained, and could care less if it were the Grim Reaper. Her heavy breathing moved the ships from her chin to her chest.

"I'm sorry."

"Fong! I'm going to kill you. You, you told Dad, didn't you? Think everything's a joke? There will be one day—"

"It's me, Cheng."

"Cheng?" She lifted her head to see Cheng standing like an angel. PaNou rubbed her red eyes. "Cheng." A warmth shot through her stomach. She grabbed the two ships.

He gently lifted her chin and then held her shoulders. Cheng's voice was calm and reassuring. "Hey." He knelt down and folded her hands into his. "The only time I ever want to see your tears again are tears of happiness. Not like this."

74

"You, you should leave now."

Cheng opened her palm to see the two tiny sticks that were their ships. "No matter what happens, we need to stick together."

PaNou nodded. "But my dad—"

"I'm not afraid of him," Cheng declared. "And you can't let him see that you're afraid of him too."

"I am afraid. I'm afraid of losing you." She looked to the ground. "I hate my life! It's like a prison."

"PaNou." Cheng held her shoulders and gazed deeply into her eyes. "You said you love me, right?"

PaNou struggled to respond. She nodded. Then she turned, facing the house. Home had never felt so threatening. What was home a few hours ago appeared now a hostile, cold structure staring right back.

The rain pranced off her thick shimmering hair.

"I don't know what to do, Cheng. Maybe death is better. At least there won't be any more suffering."

"Don't you say that! I'll always be here for you." Cheng lifted her face toward his. "Are you happy?"

She froze—shocked she had never asked herself such a simple question. "I'm, I'm not. I'm not happy here."

"Then come. Come with me." Cheng reached out both hands.

"Where will we go?"

"There's a village that's perfect for us: Tong Shia." Cheng pointed northeast where thick blankets of clouds began to depart. In the foggy distance, they could make out an enormous peak. "Behind that mountain, there is a small village where we can start a new life together. A fresh start, just you and I."

Her opened lips spoke silence.

"We can dig as many oceans as we want." There was much new energy from Cheng. With one hand, he brushed her hair. "Hey, I'll take care of you." Cheng searched into her wandering eyes. "No matter what happens, I won't ever leave you. I love you."

PaNou rose to her feet and ran her hand over her hair. Before she had a chance to respond, dishes clattered from inside the house, breaking their moment.

"Cheng, I have to go."

"What about Tong Shia?"

PaNou didn't say a word. She slightly dropped her head and walked to the house.

Was that a nod? A yes? Cheng hoped while he watched her disappear behind the layers of rain. *Why didn't she say yes? Uh, I must've sounded so stupid!* He looked over to the mountains where some areas flickered in orange balls and smoke. The raindrops, hounding his skin.

The Tiger and The Ox

The crow of a rooster called the sun out, and PaNou woke up with a residue of anger from the previous night. She lay on her bamboo bed, staring at the ceiling. Cheng consumed her mind. She had to see him again. Tiny sounds interrupted her thoughts and she could swear she heard it earlier but was too dazed in sleep. It was four knocks—*Cheng!*

Lips pressed against the wall, PaNou whispered, "Cheng?"

"Yeah. Can you come out? I want to show you something."

"How long have you been out there?"

"I don't know. An hour or so. Come out."

"What will I tell my parents? They're both up."

A moment of silence. Cheng's eyes circled.

"Wait. I got it. I'll be back."

"What?"

PaNou's footsteps faded from the wall. She walked to the living room and found her mom sewing while her father was busying himself with an opium pipe by the door. Youa looked up with wide eyes.

"This season's harvest will be bountiful with you waking up this early."

"And next year too." PaNou played along with her mom's sarcasm. "Do you have any laundry to do?"

Youa stood up—hands on her hips. "Did you finally grow up this morning?"

PaNou sighed, "I realize how much you and Dad really love us, and I just want to help more than in the past. I have two hands, too."

"Right now? I'm about to make breakfast. We can do laundry later."

"No, I want you to rest, Mom. If I take care of the laundry, then no one else will have to worry about it. By the time I'm back, breakfast will be ready."

Shaking her head, Youa replied, "I'll have to go with you. I suppose we can eat a late breakfast today."

PaNou was stumped for a moment. She thought of the long seconds Cheng was waiting outside. "Well, I thought we could maybe get two things done at the same time. How about I cook then, and you can do laundry?" She knew her mother would prefer cooking over laundry any day.

Youa laughed. PaNou didn't find it funny, but maybe it was working.

"You, cook food? I must be dreaming right now." She was laughing so loud she struggled to the front door. "Did you hear that? Your daughter said she was going to cook for us?"

Blong continued sucking and blowing into his pipe, followed with bubbly sounds. Youa mentioned it again—no reaction. He detached his lips from the pipe and gave out a long sigh. Youa shook her head. She hated being ignored.

"I will go with her." Fong jumped in. "Don't worry, Mom. I will keep an eye on her."

PaNou blew her nostrils, and echoed, "Keep an eye on who!"

"Hurry up then. I'm making something really good, so make sure you two come straight back home."

"Fong, I don't need..." PaNou stopped herself upon the realization her mom had given them permission. Her mood changed quickly. After all, she can deal with Fong personally once they get to the river. "Yes, Mom. Do you have any other clothes?"

"That's all. Make sure you check in our room. I don't know why your dad likes to take off his clothing and walk around half-naked."

"I got it," Fong volunteered. Both PaNou and Youa looked strangely at Fong.

"What's gotten into the both of you this morning?" Youa smirked.

"You mean, what's gotten into him!" PaNou shook her head.

PaNou and Fong each carried a bamboo basket of laundry. Before they walked out, PaNou ran to her room and informed Cheng to meet her at the river down the hill next to a large boulder. The two siblings began their walk with PaNou in the lead. She wanted to wait until they were far from the house before she gave him a good beating. The grass was still moist from the previous night but the morning sun was already warming their noses.

"So, Fong, you are finally smart for once because you know what is coming for you, right?" PaNou looked over her shoulder to make sure Fong was close enough to hear her.

"I know Cheng is waiting for you at the river."

"Really? How would you know because I'm stopping you right here." PaNou stomped her feet and faced her brother. "Give me the basket. I should give you a beating, but I feel like being nice to you today for once. Wait here for me. Don't move an inch, and when I'm done, we can go home together."

"Okay."

PaNou narrowed her eyes at him. "Okay? Okay. Good. You're different this morning. What do you want from me?"

"Nothing. I'm..." Fong began playing with his mouth. "I'm sorry about last night."

PaNou remained quiet but gave Fong a stare down.

"I am." Fong's brows curved back. "It wasn't really funny. I thought it would be, but I don't feel good about it. You go ahead. I'll play up the river by the fallen tree. Just come get me whenever you and Cheng are done."

Her shoulders fell back. She gave a smile to say "thank you" and looked at the two bulky baskets. "Carry this one with me to the river first." She handed Fong's basket back to him.

With another five minutes of walking, they came around a turn where the soil eroded to rocks and pebbles. Cheng surfaced from the boulder and was shocked to see Fong with PaNou. He didn't say hi, just a nod at Fong.

"Okay, don't forget to come get me." Instantly, Fong dashed up the shoreline and disappeared behind the trees.

Cheng's eyes followed Fong.

"My baby brother, I don't know what to do with him sometimes. I want to punch him but—"

"He's still very immature. I think he's learning."

Cheng then broke a smile at PaNou.

"You found this okay?"

"Yeah, my second time here, actually. A few days ago I explored some of these trails."

"Yes, this side of the river is quieter. The other side is much faster and deeper though it's great for fishing." PaNou began separating the clothing along the rocks. "Oh no, I forgot the soap."

"It's okay. I'll help you. We'll just scrub it off. That's what I do." Cheng reached forward to the other basket and began soaking them in the calm water that was mostly barricaded with rocks. "Hey, I'll be right back."

"Where are you going?"

"Keep looking at the water."

She wasn't in the mood. She bent forward and began washing the clothes. "What is it?"

"Please. Give me two minutes and keep staring at the current."

"You want me to look at the water for two minutes?" PaNou stopped dipping a white shirt. "Sure."

"Be right back." Cheng ran upriver and vanished at the turn.

What is he up to? PaNou waited for what felt like two minutes, which was really 30 seconds. As soon as she began to dip the shirt into the river again she saw vibrant colors floating downriver on an elongated bamboo boat that included pink plumerias and violet orchids. The boat carried the flowers around the turn until the waters calmed in front of her. She suddenly dropped the shirt—hands frozen in mid-wash, and her eyes began to glitter. There was a small piece of paper in the boat. She reached for it. It read:

If I had one wish, I'd wish to see the world with you.

She grabbed the boat by the bow and lifted it on-shore. The flowers were spread on the sand. No one has done anything like that for PaNou. Then the sound of jamming pebbles neared and she looked up. Cheng stood—hands drawn to the sides, and he gave her a smile. PaNou turned and bent down so her long hair curtained her eyes.

"Don't look this way."

Cheng walked around her. "I hope you like it."

"You..."

Cheng bent down to face her. "Sorry, I don't really know what flowers you like, but I—"

"Cheng." She turned opposite him. "Can you step away for a minute? Please."

"What's wrong?" Cheng looked confused. "Okay." He reached into the shallow water and began rubbing and rinsing the clothes. Except for the sound of splashing water and ripples on the soft water, there was a moment of silence. "If you tell me what flowers you like, maybe next time I can get those for you."

"It's not that." She gripped Cheng's forearm to stop him from washing. Her eyes glimmered more water than they could hold. Then a pair of blue dragonflies attached at the end buzzed by and stood on a bent grass. Together, they flew from one spot to the next. Then the pair of dragonflies took a long break on the tip of an orchid. "Do you believe in fate?"

"Fate?" Cheng looked away, pondering if he should tell her what he wants her to hear or what he truly felt.

"Honestly. Do you?"

Cheng lifted his chest. "I believe fate is when you've done everything you can to change your life and life still happens. That's fate."

81

"Well, I do." With her fingertip, she began tapping the surface of the water. The ripples shimmered until the current ate them up. "About a year ago, I dreamt I was reborn as a dragonfly. And not long ago, I had this other dream that I was on a very big boat. The kind that is bigger than a giant airplane, like a city within itself with lights, flowers, and a large place to eat....I've never even been on a boat before."

"Wow. You think a boat like that exists? Probably not. That's why it's a dream." Cheng threw two white shirts on a flat rock, soaked the rest, and replied, "The dream I remember most is about my mom. In my dream, she didn't die. She just went away for a while, and when she came back, she made me a meal every morning and made sure I never went hungry again."

"You must miss your mom very much. She did a great job."

"Great job?"

"Yeah, she raised you to be a very good man."

"Oh..." Cheng turned away. "Yeah, thanks." Cheng looked to the puffs of clouds. He couldn't even remember how she looked. She died when he was only learning to cause trouble around the house.

PaNou pulled her hair back. "I'm glad to have met you."

"Same here."

The two washed and poked fun at each other until the late morning. Afterward, Cheng went to get Fong who displayed two hand-sized fish wrapped in long grass. Cheng carried one basket while Fong carried the other.

"Did you add Cheng's clothes in here too? It feels ten times heavier," whined Fong.

"If that was the case, Cheng wouldn't have anything to wear right now," said PaNou.

"Funny. Very funny. I do have two shirts, okay. I just don't want to dirty the other one."

"You only have one shirt!" Fong laughed and almost fell backward.

82

"No. I said two, didn't I?"

"You can have this." Fong offered. PaNou quickly gave him the "stare," which he was well accustomed to. "I'm serious. It might be a bit loose on you, but it'll fit you."

"It's okay. I like mine. Thanks though."

Cheng walked back with the two siblings until Lou Sai was in sight. A few villagers walked past them, and for an odd reason each one frowned at Cheng. One of them was a woman in her mid-forties but looked twenty years older. She wore a constant droopy expression.

"PaNou!" said the woman.

"Hi, Auntie." The woman was not PaNou's blood aunt, but it was courteous to refer to her with such title.

"Him! Who is he?" The woman studied Cheng whose pants were wet and smeared with dirt.

"He's my friend, Cheng," Fong answered. Cheng and PaNou were surprised but impressed with the response.

"Your parents are highly respected around here. Please don't let the world know. People will ridicule you, but when they do, they won't say your name. Instead, they'll mention your mom and dad's name."

A week passed, and news of Cheng and PaNou had spread like wildfire through the network of Hmong villages. Cheng and PaNou's trouble became the dessert of every meal and such news disturbed the Lee elders greatly. Many of them pressed Xai Lee, a small man in stature but one who was a well-respected shaman with a blunt personality. Such a man was one of a few who could make Blong listen.

"Blong, you are an intelligent man. But an intelligent man is judged not only by what he does but also by the situation he puts himself into. You must resolve this dilemma soon."

"They sent you here, didn't they? Those old men worry too much."

Xai returned Blong a cold stare because he too was an "old man."

83

"I've got this under control."

"Blong, every Hmong I know respects you and that's why we chose you to lead the Lee Clan." While he spoke, he never once blinked, locking his eyes on Blong who was pacing back and forth. "This news of your daughter isn't good for us at all. It's making our Lee Clan look bad. True or not, we are losing face to the other clans. I don't care if he's an orphan or prince; their animal spirits are simply not compatible."

Blong blew his nostrils.

"These stories of her spending time with this orphan will not only ruin our clan, but ruin your name. Why, if my memory hasn't failed me I remember it was you, Mr. Blong Lee who famously said, 'It takes a generation to raise a good life but one life to ruin a generation.' You must not let this continue or else no man will ever want to wed your daughter. She is starting to have a dirty reputation." Xai stretched his mouth, and then continued, "I already see that less people are coming to visit you these days."

"I said I have this under control. I'll handle it to-night."

"I hope you take my words seriously. If they marry, I'm afraid the worst has yet to come to them, and to your family. Don't forget, I am a shaman after all. Their animal spirits are the most dangerous I've ever come across in my seventy years—"

The door opened, and in walked Blong's oldest son, Tou, and behind him was a young and very nervous girl. Blong's thin eyebrows elevated. His lips opened.

"Dad," Tou said with a small grin. He pulled the girl to his side.

Blong was not in the mood. He tightened his lips and blew his nostrils, and looked to the girl. "You must be Wa Her's daughter. You are what, fifteen years old?"

"Thirteen." She nodded, timidly.

"Go home. Right now. This is the worst time for you to be here—"

She clung to Tou, frightened like a little kitten.

"Dad, why are you treating my wife like this?"

"She's not your wife. Not until we do the wedding, and that is *if* we do the wedding." Blong turned his eyes to the girl and addressed her, "The day you can wake up before my rooster is the day when you will marry my son. Go home. Tell your dad I'll send him some money tomorrow morning for this—this inconvenience, and if anyone asks you never stepped in my house, you hear?"

Tou interrupted, "But Dad, I already brought her into the house—"

"Shut your mouth right now. You are my oldest son, and I'll pick the right wife for you."

The girl and Tou looked at each other for a moment. She tugged her hand away and left.

"They grow up fast, don't they?" Xai mumbled. "Well, think about what I said. I'll come back in a few days."

"So be it." Blong combed his hand over his balding forehead, turning his attention to his son. "Tou—"

"Dad, I'm twenty-five years old. I don't want to wait until I'm an old man—"

"I'm your father and so long as I am your father you are to listen to me. Let me deal with PaNou and that orphan boy she can't live without first. Afterward, we can talk about finding a wife for you."

"You're talking about Cheng?" Tou saw the immense frustration on his father's face. "Dad, if you truly keep your words, then don't worry about Cheng. I'll take care of him for you."

"You kids—there's no need to get involved in this." Blong gave his oldest son a stern look and emphasized, "That girl of yours, she's a Her. Remember the Her Clan, they can be very cruel."

The following evening PaNou sat on a wooden stool in the living room, sewing a front panel apron. She inserted bright green beads through another needle. That was when Blong rampaged in.

"My daughter, you need to listen very well. You've seen what happened to your older sister for doing things her own way. Now Ka is a slave to her husband who beats her every single day."

"It's her life."

"If you stick with Cheng, yours will be much worse. Is that the kind of life you want?"

PaNou wanted to ignore her father. She inserted the needle in and out of a cloth. "I'm not going to have a life like *that*."

Losing his patience, Blong's small hands waved with each word. "Do you know that because of *you*, I've been losing face? People used to respect me and our family."

"They can think whatever they want—I don't care. I'm not living my life for them."

"I care! You must realize that this Cheng of yours rides the Ox and you ride the Tiger. Oxen and Tigers are not destined to be together. In fact, they can't be together. Even a brainless person only *needs* to be told this once."

PaNou stopped sewing, and her eyes blurred with tears.

"Let me tell you once more. Each individual who is born rides a certain animal spirit to this earth. Animal spirits have preferences. The right match brings the highest chance of a fruitful marriage, a happy life. Your spirit and Cheng's are the worst I've ever seen. If you marry him, you probably won't live very long!"

"I don't care. Everyone dies sooner or later. Besides, they're just stories," she replied. PaNou was having a difficult time focusing on her needlework. "People can be with whomever they wish."

"Your body may be big, but you still think like a kid. This isn't a fairy tale. This is reality. It doesn't matter what you think or what I think. This is the Law of Life!"

"I don't care about your 'Law of Life.'"

Blong puffed his chest, shaking his head. "It's not my rules. One day you'll realize every place, every life, every

86

spirit has its own set of rules. You break the rules—you pay a *big* price."

"Whatever." She frowned, and grabbed a small scissors to cut the thread, redoing what she had sewn.

"Yeah, keep that attitude up." Blong closed his eyes for a few seconds to maintain his temper. It was a technique Youa had taught him. "PaNou, you know who suffers the most?—It's not you. It's me."

"You have no idea what you're putting me through."

"It's all about you, right? You and your selfish thinking. People aren't tearing apart your name. It's *my* name, *my* face!" He towered over PaNou. "As long as I am your father, I will not allow you to marry him."

"I don't want you as my father," whispered PaNou. "We're just dating right now, anyway."

"PaNou, listen to your father," Youa rushed in from the dining room with lettuce leaves still in one hand.

"Why are you both so against me?" PaNou looked up at her parents. "I can't do anything here! My life is nothing but hell. Every day it's wash the dishes, clean the house, do the laundry. And then again, wash the dishes, clean the house—I'm so sick of this life! No matter what I do, it's never good enough!" PaNou threw the needlework down.

"Bring me the whip."

"She's not a kid anymore." Youa gave Blong a stern look—then turned to PaNou. "You are a daughter with good genes. Tall and beautiful. All you still need are good senses." She studied the lettuce leaves in her hand, and made eye contact with PaNou again. "You see this lettuce? Men are like lettuce. Many of them are the same. You have to pick one and be happy with it. But, Cheng, he isn't a good lettuce. I'll help you find a better one. In fact, you should meet—"

"No, Mom. You both don't understand—"

"I'm sure she'll understand the whip better." Blong walked off to the living room. Youa rushed to her husband. They had a quick conversation and she returned to PaNou.

"Don't speak anymore. Your father is very angry. And we don't want people to hear all about this."

"But—"

"I know you're big now, and I can't control you. Like your dad, the both of you are very stubborn. I've been with your dad for almost thirty years. Sometimes he still doesn't listen."

"Then why are you with him, Mom?"

Youa opened a smile. She had always enjoyed sharing stories of her and Blong. "Because your dad loves me very much," she said. "Like many couples, we had our own troubles at the start." For a moment, flashbacks overcame her. "My father forced us to marry. Then, I was only fifteen—younger than you. Many of my friends said I was too pretty for him and that he was too old. I learned to really love your father." Her face brightened. "Believe it or not, your father, he can be sweet at times. He used to sing to me a lot," she sighed, briefly reliving those good memories. "He taught me that no matter how much you try to block a river, it will find its way through."

PaNou stood up. "Then why don't you understand me, Mom? Cheng, he loves me very much."

"If that's truly where your love flows, I guess...I can't stop you. I'm very worried—"

"That I don't know what I'm doing?"

"Yes, marriage should only happen once, you know."

The distressed PaNou simply nodded her head.

"Your father and I want to make sure you have the best life possible."

"But, Mom—"

"Go to your bed now before your father comes back. We'll talk tomorrow."

PaNou grabbed her needlework, crossed her arms, and walked to her room.

For the next two days, Blong began an onslaught of rumors to surrounding villages that Cheng was a crook like his father. He began telling locals to keep Cheng away from Lou

Sai, and if they saw him, to inform Blong. Every time Cheng's name was mentioned, Blong roared with rage.

"You marry that thief and I'll no longer have you as my daughter!"

"He's a good man," PaNou said. Her comments were useless as Blong crushed her soft words with his barking. She defended, "You just don't know him."

"Are you blind? Look at yourself! That crook has stolen your heart *and* your brain, too." Blong, who was angrier than he'd ever been slammed the front door open. "So you really want to be with him?"

PaNou didn't answer. Instead, she gave her father the meanest look her pretty face could create.

"Then get out of my house. RIGHT NOW!"

"You're a bit too harsh," Youa intervened.

"No. This must be done. It's the only way she'll learn." Blong turned to PaNou. "Listen. If it weren't for your mother, I would've kicked you out a long time ago like the dog you are! So you better thank your mother because I'm giving you one last chance to think really hard about this."

PaNou stood, unmoved. Then she started trembling. Such words from her own father pierced her like a thousand arrows. She sat on the floor and hid her face in her arms. The choice was evident: It was either Cheng or her family. By not taking a position, she was devastating both. The pressure from her family and clan crushed her. Such effort to forget about Cheng was useless. The harder PaNou tried to move on, the more she missed him.

Despite the oppression against their unity, Cheng had shown a wealth of unconditional love to her. Such love, PaNou couldn't deny. Plus, the way her father was forcing his ways, she wanted to get away. Anywhere. The more her parents tried to take charge of her life, the more she thought about Cheng. If only they would give her a chance to explain, things would be different.

Blong walked to the kitchen, preaching his words to Youa. "Deep in his heart, I know Cheng's a cruel person. He's manipulated PaNou." Blong grabbed a few slices of mango and began chewing them. "I don't understand how our daughter could like someone like him—short as a stump, uneducated, poor, and no one likes the guy. I tried liking him, and it only makes me hate him."

"I don't know what else to say," Youa responded. She stared into space, uninterested in the vegetables she was preparing.

"Remember the trip to Dae Lia?"

Youa's lips shriveled.

"I was wrong about PaNou. She's not as dumb as a pig—she's ten times dumber. At least a pig knows fear from its owner—"

"Let her be—"

"No." Blong said, standing taller. "I will not let those two marry. Cheng *is* bad luck. I mean, look! His mother died at nineteen when he was only five years old. Then he and his father were robbed—they lost their entire herd of cattle. Cheng then stole his neighbor's chickens, got caught, and was fined. His father was thrown in jail! And when Cheng's father returned, he didn't want anything to do with the boy. His own father doesn't even want to acknowledge him!"

"That's Kou Yang, right?"

"Yes!"

"Isn't he a teacher?"

"They kicked him out, and now he's the most famous thief. It's in their blood. Father and son are from one seed." Blong turned to face the sobbing PaNou. "See, good people make mistakes, but they learn from them. Bad people like Cheng only become the mistake. That thief! He'll do more good being dead."

PaNou rushed to the kitchen to plead her case. PaNou fought back her tears and boldly, she confronted her father.

"Cheng just had a few bad things happened to him, but if you give him a chance, he's a really good person."

"Brainwashed!" Blong said, angrily.

"PaNou, listen to us. We're just worried about your future," Youa comforted.

"Listen. Men, there are plenty of them. We'll find a very good man for you. If you think Cheng is a good man, the others you'll see are a million times better," said Blong.

Furious, PaNou took a deep breath. "Stop it! Stop controlling my life. Please! I see how you two are, and I don't want my life to be like yours."

"PaNou, watch your tongue," Youa ceased her slicing, and she pushed the green onions aside. "Don't forget that at least we have a nice house, money, and none of you kids are starving. No one in this house has to go begging for anything."

"I've never seen you two say anything nice to each other—like how much you love each other. You two are always arguing. I've heard you, Mom, praying for your boyfriend to come back, and Dad calling for his Mai Gao."

"PaNou!" Youa held her chin high. "What's so special about Cheng that you can't let go? Don't tell me you're pregnant?"

"What! Mom, how could you say that to me?" Frustrated, PaNou shut her eyes and screamed, "Of course, I'm not!"

"Then why?" Youa crossed her arms.

PaNou's eyes raced across the floor. "I-I love him."

Blong groaned.

Youa continued, "And Cheng?"

Blong grabbed his face. He was speechless, twisting his body as much as his head in displeasure.

"Mom, Cheng loves me. Deep in my heart, I know no one else will love me as much as him."

Youa looked at her daughter and dipped her head before slicing more onions.

"Exactly!" Blong punched the air with inflamed eyes. "Love is what poisoned you! Oh, I'm warning you. Don't you marry for love. Your family and clan is the real love you're searching for—right here. You see, there are two types of orphans. Some are born as orphans and some are abandoned like Cheng, because no one wants him."

"I want him," whispered PaNou.

Blong's face was beet red, and he turned to face his wife. "My goodness. I guess it's impossible to talk sense to a pig. Why aren't you telling your daughter?"

"She's also your daughter, Old Man."

Turning to PaNou with his eyes wide open, Blong yelled, "PaNou, you have disgraced me! Are you truly blind! Why am I wasting my words here!—Even his own father doesn't want him. No father would do that to his son." Blong began rocking his head. "And you say Cheng is a good man. Oh, PaNou, you've yet to grow up. That lazy orphan has no friends, no family. He can't even take care of himself, so how's he going to take care of you?—He can't! Cheng's actually a smart man because he has you trapped." Blong pointed to his mouth as he spoke, "Mark my words, you'll be his slave and suffer the rest of your life for him." Blong turned to his wife before walking away. "Why is your daughter so stupid?"

"Must be your seeds," Youa said.

Without a response, Blong stomped away.

Misfortunes

What Blong spoke of did have some truth behind it. Sadly, for Cheng, many of his unfortunate events were out of his control. Such misfortunes started years before Cheng met PaNou. The first tragedy occurred when his mother, who seemed perfectly healthy at the time, died unexpectedly. No cause was ever known. To make things worse, Cheng's father, Kou, remarried immediately after the funeral. Rumors spread that Kou had poisoned his wife. Kou denied the allegations but then quickly took off, abandoning his only child, Cheng, who at the time was left alone in the midst of the chaos.

Over the years and until Cheng met PaNou, the new stepmother never grew a liking for Cheng. In fact, the only things that grew were her hatred for him—plus the size of her waist. So, while PaNou battled wars within her own clan, Cheng continued to free himself of slavery from his stepmother. The stepmother was like an oversized thug, wearing sparkling clothing along with belts of countless fake silver coins.

Cheng simply called her "Fat Woman," who arrogantly accepted the name. Fat Woman was frightening in her own oddities. Big-chested and hairy, she wore the thickest layer of foundation. The brilliant pinkish-white color of her face clearly clashed against the pale yellow color of her stout neck. Wide throughout, her colorful skirt, coin belts, and colorful hat made her look like a giant ball from a circus. When she moved, she had to kick and plant her tiny legs to prevent herself from rolling.

Fat Woman's favorite thing to say to Cheng was "Oh, my son, are you a good person, or a bad person?"

Without hesitation, Cheng would always answer, "Good person."

She'd then continue, "If you're a good person, then wash the dishes *now*." It went from cleaning the dishes to doing the laundry, massaging her calves, and anything else the woman's tiny head could imagine.

Cheng quickly caught on to her cruel methods. Such reverse psychology had evidently worked on Cheng's father, Kou, who essentially became a pet, obeying every desire of Fat Woman. Together, his father and stepmother coerced Cheng at a young age to do work that rivaled a slave—performing a variety of taxing chores, such as cooking, cleaning the utensils, and attending the farm alone while his father spent all day with Fat Woman. This deeply aggravated the relationship between Cheng and Kou, so much Cheng no longer acknowledged Kou as his father.

With the rising trouble of PaNou's parents and grueling years of being the sole laborer, Cheng lived in constant depression. He wasn't the kind who liked to fight back against anyone, particularly his parent, but eventually Cheng had enough of the tormenting, and so he spent the following days planning a retaliation.

One day after Cheng returned later than normal from the farm he saw the large glitzy lady singing and waiting for him in front of the house. It was also the only day Cheng skipped his chores. The dishes and food were left in the exact place they were after breakfast. Flies swarmed the table and plates. That day he didn't attend the farm and instead, he left to play at a nearby creek after visiting PaNou.

Arms barely crossed over her large chest, Fat Woman's eyes surveyed his return. Though she was able to break a smile, Cheng knew it was a cover-up. Behind the sweet smile was pure malevolence.

Cheng was prepared for a verbal battle and sensed her rage. She tried to intimidate him by stuffing her small chin into her chest, creating two more layers. He contained himself from laughing at such effort as he walked into the house.

"My son, today you must've worked so hard at the farm. Look, it's almost sunset. You must be exhausted."

"I am tired, but I don't mind doing it again tomorrow." Cheng, of course, had better plans than the farm.

"Now, my boy, do you want to be a good person, or a bad person?"

Here we go again, Cheng thought while he sat on a stool.

The large woman displayed the same sinister expression every time she asked the question. Cheng was prepared for her mind game this time and decided to answer differently. For Cheng's sake, it took much courage.

"Why aren't you answering me? Do you want to be a good person, or—"

"I want to be a bad person."

"Okay, if you want to be a good person…" There was a choking pause. Appalled, his stepmother coughed, nearly suffocating. "S-so you want to be a *bad person!*" Her tiny eyes enlarged and yet were still puny, and her body doubled its size, only stopping at the pressure of her tightly knotted sash.

"I don't want to be a good person anymore. Being a bad person is the best. Mom, what about you? Do you want to be a good or bad person?"

"Oh, always a good person," said Fat Woman, happily. "My son—"

"Then you should always cook, wash the dishes, and clean the house. Oh, and also tend the farm." Cheng smirked, looking her directly in the eyes. He dropped his large bamboo basket in front of her. "Here you go. Like you always told me, good people are hard to find." He charged out and joined in a chasing game with the next-door kids.

The following day, an angry Kou came looking for Cheng at the farm but he was nowhere to be found. One of the neighboring farmers informed Kou he had seen Cheng walking to the nearby creek. Kou followed a fresh trail of bent grass. After a short walk, he hid behind a tree and found Cheng below, wading in the creek.

The large creek flowed gently, massaging over large rocks. Its sound drummed against the stones and ruffled hanging branches nearby. Lush green vegetation and plants bordered its serenity. Sitting on a giant rock, Cheng kicked and splashed.

For once, Cheng was enjoying solitude. Eyes closed, he stopped splashing and listened to the placid rippling. He breathed the freshness of the mountain-fed water into his lungs and reopened his eyes. *Things will be okay,* Cheng told himself. He bent forward to study his face on the slow-moving surface. *Hey, you're not bad luck. You're the luckiest man alive. You're with a beautiful and kind girl named, PaNou. Everything will be okay.*

A set of stones someone had placed in a circle by the bank reminded Cheng of the rainy evening when they played "ocean." He knelt down and cupped the sparkling water. Tilting his palms, he released the water between his fingers—drop by drop. Softly, Cheng whispered, "Let this water carry our love, far away where no one will find us."

Suddenly, the imminent sound of shuffling grass scared him. He jumped to his feet. For a second, Cheng feared a panther. There, in the tall green needle grass was his father.

"My son. We live a short life in this world." Kou walked closer. "Remember, women—there are plenty of them, but you will only have *one* dad."

Cheng sat calmly on the large rock and continued to stare at the flowing stream.

"There is a girl not too far from here; her name is Chia Vang. They say she is a very hard worker."

"She does sound very good. So why don't you go marry her instead of Fat Woman?"

"My son—"

"You keep saying 'my son,' 'my son,' but I know you don't care about me."

"You should respect your father. I raised you—"

"No, you didn't. When Mom died, you left me all by myself so you could chase Fat Woman who does nothing but eat." Cheng looked at his rough hands. "I had to beg others for food, cleaned their clothing—I could've died and you wouldn't have noticed."

"When you get older, you'll realize that we as humans sometimes say and do things we don't mean."

"I know, but you never acknowledged what you did. You never apologized. What—you expect me to forget about it and pretend like nothing happened? Then you walk over me like dirt. Over and over again. People can forgive, but they'll always remember." Cheng threw his hands up. "I had to eat other people's trash for two months!" His eyes flickered.

"I hear you've been seeing a Lee girl, PaNou. I am your father, and I don't approve of her at all. I think you deserve better."

"When did it matter to you?"

"I won't let you marry her." Kou slanted his head to one side, but kept his menacing eyes at Cheng. "I've been warned twice by the Lee Clan."

"Yeah. Well, I've been kicked and punched. So what's new?" Cheng splashed the creek with a stone.

"Did you forget that our own clan abandoned us years ago? Just when they accepted me back and were beginning to respect my name, you have to chase that brat PaNou!"

"Respect? Look at yourself!" Cheng said, trying to compose himself. "They disrespect us because of you and Fat Woman. I don't know why you even like her. She's more of a man than you—she has more moustache than you."

"There are many women out there, far better and more beautiful than your skinny spoiled brat."

"That brat you keep talking about has a name, all right?" Cheng was growing irritated his father's choices of words. If Kou wasn't his biological dad, he would've punched him senseless.

"Are you stupid or smart? There are plenty of women around!"

"You keep saying that so why don't you find someone new?"

Kou looked away, perplexed.

"While you and Fat Woman go out and play, I've been turned into a slave." Shaking his head at his father, Cheng glared with a painful look. "You don't love me. You never did."

"If I didn't, then why am I wasting my time with you? Do you realize that people are already bashing my name out there?"

Cheng took a deep breath.

"They're about to fine me ten silver bars and two cows. You hear! They'll ruin us. Listen carefully—do not see PaNou anymore. I'll take you over to see Chia today," Kou smiled. Drawing her round figure with his hands he continued, "She's very pretty and she's got meat."

"Unlike you, there's only one woman in my heart."

"My son, you need to get around more. See more people."

"If that's the case, then get rid of Fat Woman."

"I'm really wasting breath here." Kou turned and left.

Cheng returned his attention to the creek.

Kou arrived home to his wife. Fat Woman looked like she had crawled out of a dumpster with her long dark hair scattered about her body. The house on the other hand, never looked so organized.

"What happened?" Kou questioned, but was more intrigued at how different the house looked.

Fat Woman leaned all her weight against Kou who nearly fell backward. She whimpered, dramatizing it.

"What's going on?"

"It's your lazy son! He forced me to work for him. He said if I didn't, he'd beat me with a stick."

"No, I won't let anybody hurt you," Kou said, hugging her.

"Your son told me that he hates me. Said we're too controlling. I tried to love him so much."

Kou kissed her plump hand. "Don't worry. I'll give him my final warning later today."

"No. No!" Fat Woman screamed. "My heart can't bear this anymore. If you want him, then I'm leaving," she threatened, fixing her hair.

"Wait—"

"I'll be with mom and dad. Did you forget I'm a daughter of a wealthy family?" Without giving him a look, she trotted out the door. "Think carefully before you come find me."

A few hours later, Cheng returned home to find Kou home alone. It was the first time in many years that Fat Woman wasn't with him. Something grave was bothering Kou. Cheng knew it was because of their earlier argument.

"Why are you so crazy for that brat?"

"I don't know...if you're talking about PaNou, it's because she's a good person," Cheng said, holding his anger. Really though, Cheng wanted to ask his father a similar question back but didn't want to create further conflict.

"Of course, she is. That brat hails from the most re-spected clan. But you, yes, you are a fool!" He kicked the stool, sending it crashing wildly into the wall. "It shows that you still act like a kid. You are blind. No matter how many times I tell you, you can't see it. She's playing with you. Think about it." Cheng's father walked to the open front door and leaned against the wall. "Seriously, what kind of girl would like a lazy, short person like you?"

"You shouldn't say that—" Cheng muttered.

"No," interrupted his father, "you *listen* to me. I am your father. I know you've never listened to me before because I probably haven't been hard enough on you. That PaNou of yours will bring more trouble and I'll have to deal with it. Do you understand—I don't even have the face to walk out of this house anymore!"

"Why is everyone so against us?"

"Because a poor and scrawny boy like you and a dumb man like me, we are not supposed to associate ourselves with them. We're different breeds." Pointing his finger at Cheng, Kou deepened his voice. "I'll make it simple for you. It's like this: You and I are like dogs and they are like horses. I'm sure you don't see horses and dogs getting married."

"If you want to use those words then *yeah*, I've seen a dog and horse together. You and Fat Woman make a great example."

"I gave birth to you and this is the respect you give back? One day your son will do the same thing to you. Of course, you don't care because the Lee Clan is not coming after you. They're coming after me. They will curse my name to my grave."

With great difficulty, Cheng kept quiet, as it was the best way to keep his father from bashing him further.

"You know what? I don't care anymore! I don't have to be here. Look at this dump." Their house was empty except for two stools, a flat bed made from bamboo, and scattered in one corner were a few pots and pans. One pan still had crusted food from a few days ago. Opposite the pots and pans was a thin navy blue cloth with holes—Cheng's blanket.

"Easy for you. You have Fat Woman and her rich family."

"Well, then you must obey my words, for I am your father."

"You never acted like one." It was painful for Cheng to say those words. He fought back his tears because he didn't want to show any sign of weakness. Cheng continued, "Anyone should have the right to be with whomever they love. You don't like it when I tell you to get rid of Fat Woman—"

"You don't get it, do you? Do you have ten silver bars? Of course, you don't." There was a moment of silence between the two. Suddenly, he mocked, "Even if you were to marry PaNou, you don't even have the dowry."

"Me? How could you ask me? As a father, the dowry is your job. You wasted all the money on opium and your new wife. I know you never cared about my future."

"So now you're the father and I'm the son? Choose your words carefully—for one day you will have many sons and then you'll realize life is not as easy as it looks—"

"Then don't make it any harder!" Cheng looked up at his father. "I know you still have some money left."

"Really? Where is it then?"

"It's what you're smoking every day." Cheng looked at the large bamboo pipe by the door.

"It's free. I got it from a *friend*, something you don't have."

"I know you're saving to buy yourself another wife." Cheng rubbed his nose. "But the truth is Fat Woman is just using you."

"Who brought you into this world? How could you speak so low to me?"

"We're going in circles. Forget it! I can work and earn it myself."

"Remember, I *am* your father. Without me there *is* no you."

"You're not my father. My real father, he died a long time ago," Cheng said, looking away.

"Is that so? You want to be your own man? You've got your wish!"

Cheng held back a volcanic explosion of anger from erupting. Looking at the dirt floor tears trickled down his dry cheeks.

"Oh, my poor son is crying. How *sad*."

Cheng turned his back on his father, confirming that he no longer respected him.

"It wouldn't be like this if Mom was here."

"What did you say?" Kou shouted.

"You poisoned Mom, didn't you?" Cheng turned his head and looked Kou in the eyes.

Kou began to shake violently. With no further words, he stormed to the bedroom, pushing a stash of clothing into a small bag. With a sickle in one hand, he stopped at the door. "You keep blaming your bad fortunes on me! Now here's your chance to be your own man! You HEAR! Who cares about an animal like you anyway! From this day on, I am no longer your father and you are no longer my son!"

In an instant, Cheng's father was gone. There was no goodbye. No last look. Only the last words, "No longer my son." echoed in his mind. Clapping footsteps faded into the distance. Cheng didn't know what to do next. Like a gargoyle, he sat frozen, trying to make sense of what had just transpired.

Once the sounds of Kou's footsteps disappeared, Cheng slowly walked to the doorway. There, he saw his father's figure pass down the dirt road. He watched. The tall shadow shrunk until it was gone behind a bend. Mixed feelings of anger, disappointment, and resentment fell upon him. He wanted to cry but for what? Over the past seven years his father was never there for him. Still, his knees buckled, and he dropped. Then he broke into a silent cry. The laughter of children stole Cheng's mind, momentarily. A few houses up the road the hunched Nhia Bee wobbled, waving his fist as fast as his mouth.

"Jay, oh, Jay! Give the ball to Moua! Right now!" shouted the old man.

Jay, the older sibling only increased the teasing of his younger brother. Nhia Bee tried chasing the older boy but lost his balance and fell flat on his back. Like a tortoise he twisted, kicked, and turned to stand.

Jay zipped around like a squirrel, stopping only to watch his fallen grandpa. He handed the ball to his younger brother and the two boys joined in the hilarity. Nhia Bee slid to his side. Finally, with lots more twisting he found his way on his feet—still yelling at Jay.

Such a sight reminded Cheng of how badly he wanted his own family, his own love. It brought a smile that washed away his present anguish. Love and family meant more than anything else in the world, and it started with PaNou. With his mind set Cheng was determined to find a way. Once again, Tong Shia echoed in his mind.

As days went by, Blong had taken new measures to separate PaNou from Cheng. They sent more men over to Cheng's house, but the orphan wasn't there. During the daytime two men stayed watch at the Lee's residence. All the effort did was ingrain fortitude in Cheng.

While PaNou faced daily lectures and sometimes threats from family and friends, Cheng fared worse. He became infamous as the orphan boy with bad luck. Nearly everyone he encountered ridiculed him and in a short time, he grew tired of absorbing verbal attacks so he began retaliating with words. On one particular occasion, he swung with fists—and a mango. This occurred on an early afternoon at a crowded street market.

The day at the marketplace in Lou Sai was humid and sunny. High in the open sky a bomber plane painted two white lines. Villagers and shoppers alike crowded the roadside bazaar, oblivious to the large jet soaring high above. PaNou's three brothers, Tou, Kang, and Fong were shopping for lychee and other fruits when Tou recognized the round face and sloping shoulders of Cheng. They shoved their way through the crowded market and hunted him down.

"Look! It's Cheng," Tou announced. He had been tracking down Cheng for days, and seeing Cheng at the market was merely coincidence. The three brothers approached him. "Cheng!"

Cheng looked around before he saw two bodies shoving toward him. He recognized Tou's face and from his pestering look, he sensed trouble. A week prior, he suffered a warning attack by Tou and his group of friends. Nonetheless, Cheng respectfully greeted him. Meanwhile, Fong fell back behind the crowd.

"Hey, nice to see you," Cheng said.

"Shut your mouth, Mother Buffalo!" Kang punched his fists together.

"Cheng, Cheng, I told you before not to see my sister, but you don't listen, do you? You know, all because of *you*, our family's breaking apart. You better not see her anymore, hear me!" Tou began circling his shoulders.

"I don't want any trouble," Cheng said, calmly.

"I guess you'll listen better to my fists. We'll have to beat you harder this time." Tou's eyes sat deep under the shadows of his brows, giving him a natural menacing look.

"Just leave him alone," said Fong, and he began walking away from the scene.

"Get back here, Fong," said Kang.

Cheng stood motionless, arms dropped to his sides and eyes glued on Tou. "Hey guys, I *really* don't want any trouble here."

"Too late, Fart Face," said Kang. "You see our sister, you see our fists!" He aimed his fist directly at Cheng.

Some people forfeited their shopping and began to crowd around the boys.

"I can see whoever I want," replied Cheng while he continued looking down at the yellow-red mango in his hand. Then he stopped rolling the mango, and gripped it.

"Hey, son! You buying that?" the owner asked.

"Nah, he can't even afford the skin," Tou sneered.

"Man, you sure stink like cow dung! Does an orphan know what bathing is?" shouted Kang, who was the shortest of the three brothers. He continued, "You must be a mixed breed between a chicken and a boar." Some bystanders found it funny and laughed.

All at once, the entire world appeared to be laughing at Cheng. He felt the burning glares from everyone and his body boiled.

Tou and Kang continued to enjoy their time scoffing. Unable to remain calm any longer, Cheng erupted like a volcano. He shot the mango directly at Kang's face, knocking him senseless on his back with his feet kicking to the sky. In a blink of an eye, Tou charged at Cheng. Rather than running away, Cheng launched a barrel of straight punches. Tou ate a straight knuckle followed by two others—one to the nose and the other to his loud mouth where he nearly swallowed Cheng's whole fist. While falling forward, Tou tackled Cheng to the ground and scratched his face. Then the crowd separated the two and stifled the scuffle.

The following evening, Cheng almost decided not to visit PaNou. He was hurt—more emotionally than physically. Still, Cheng made the effort to visit, and like his spirit, the night was hazy.

Once every few minutes, a depressed amber moon would peek out from the clouds to witness the young couple's chatter. Because there were now guards at watch until darkness, Cheng didn't make his visit nor play his ncas until they left.

Cheng gave a few light knocks on her wall.

"Hey, you came?" Her sweet voice had a healing power that cooled Cheng's burning scratch. "I heard what happened today. I'm so sorry for—"

"It's not your fault."

"Are you okay?"

"Yeah."

The fight with her brothers left a pain deeper than the bloody scratch under his eye. Cheng wanted to forget about what happened because he might cry. Then there was the flashback of his father and him separating. Everything was piling up on him.

"It's a quiet night," Cheng said, though he could hear the pain across his face as loud as a scream.

"Everyone's asleep," PaNou replied. "Aren't you scared of the dark?"

"It's okay. It's the only time when there aren't any guards." Cheng drew a match and lit a small candle.

"My father's really gone crazy. I'm afraid."

"Afraid of what?"

"If they catch you…I don't know what I'll do."

"They won't catch me."

"Well, my dad's planning to get a few dogs."

Cheng breathed heavily, and he stared at the glittering stars. Surrounding him was complete darkness except for the tips of the nearest leaves that reflected a golden glow from the candlelight. Even with the light there was a sense of trepidation. The pitch darkness behind the bamboo reminded Cheng of ghost tales his father used to tell. Speaking with his eyes affixed to the stars, Cheng cared less if the monsters from the ghost stories came out and mauled him. He needed to talk to PaNou. To hear her sweet voice was worth it.

"So how was your day?"

"Mmm...okay. I thought you weren't going to come."

"Hey, you know I always come."

"I'm very worried. My dad's been trying to find your dad, and when he does, he'll press a fine against him."

"Ah, it doesn't matter. I never had a dad."

"What happened? Did you two get into another argument?"

Cheng sighed, "We did. It was really bad. He left me for good—with his new wife."

PaNou gasped.

"Now, I'm officially an orphan."

"Please don't say that."

"It'll be for the better," Cheng said, holding his hands together. "I missed you a lot, Sweetheart."

"Sweetheart? That's a new word." She blushed.

"You don't mind me calling you 'Sweetheart,' do you?"

"I don't. I guess I'm not used to it yet."

"Then I'll say it more often."

"All right, I'll call you...Honey then."

She turned to the wall and pressed her open palms to the wall. "Put your hands against the wall." She quietly tapped so Cheng could follow where her hand was from outside. Eyes closed, she smiled.

"Will you ever leave me?"

"I'll never leave you," Cheng replied.

"A lot of things have been happening. We can't keep doing this. I mean, once my dad gets his dogs there's no way we can keep doing this." PaNou paused. She thought of Cheng's proposition of leaving to Tong Shia, and asked, "Do you truly love me like you say you do?"

"Why do you keep asking me that?" Cheng felt offended as though he hasn't shown enough, especially by taking those beatings. "Sweetheart, you know I love you with all my heart."

"I want to be with you."

Cheng pressed his face against the wall. "Me, too."

"Hey, Honey?"

"Yeah…"

"Kang came in crying today. He had this huge bruise on his face and told me you and your big friend attacked them."

"Hah. He means my big friend, Mango." Cheng laughed, quietly. "I threw a mango at him. Maybe I shouldn't have, it was a *nice* mango."

"That must've hurt."

"Well, I feel bad but they made a laughing stock of me in public. Tou scratched me like a girl. I didn't mean to…I did say 'hi' to them at first—"

"Just forget about them."

There was silence between the couple.

"We need to get out of here." The two spoke the same words at the same time.

"Honey, a lot of people don't like us and it hurts me when people call you names."

"It's okay. I'm fine. I can handle myself."

"I know you love me very much, and I'm going to find a way to make things right."

"We'll *both* find a way," Cheng smiled. He stared at the candle's flickering flame. "Everything will be okay."

The Escape

On the wooden table, Youa served boiled chicken flavored with one of her special broths for a late lunch. Blong was tearing the chicken into smaller parts, giving Fong a wing and thigh. Fong grabbed the stool beside his father and after dipping the wing in a small bowl of pepper and fish sauce, he began chewing on it.

"Where are your two brothers?"

"They went to spin tops, and they didn't want me to go. They don't want me to hang out with them ever again." Fong gave his father a sad face, hoping he'd feel sorry for him—

PaNou walked in the kitchen, tossed a few strips of chicken on a plate of rice, and drifted to the living room.

"Aren't you eating with us?" Youa looked over.

PaNou continued her tiny steps without a word.

"Bring your mouth over here and eat with the family!" Blong demanded.

"I can eat wherever I want."

Youa brought a bowl of sliced cucumbers to the table. Next to it, she placed a small plate of salt and smashed green pepper. "Let her be."

Blong shook his head sideways. He quickly swallowed a piece of chicken and stepped to the front door and slammed it shut. Standing above PaNou, he said, "This *love* you keep mentioning—oh, my daughter, when you have a family, you don't care about love. What you care about is having food on the table. I've seen people marry for love, and they ended up killing each other. I told you about Malee. She married her *Love*, and what did her Love do to her? One day, he sliced her throat while she slept. *You* are walking right in that path."

"Dad! Why are you always cursing me?"

"I am only telling you the truth." Blong rubbed his oily lips. "That Cheng of yours, I'll catch him and when I do, I'll make sure he never, ever, sees you again."

PaNou had begun eating but now had lost her appetite. She set her plate on another stool—then looked directly at her father, and yelled, "You keep saying Cheng's a bad person, well, look at yourself! Don't you ever hear your own words? No wonder I've been losing my mind."

Blong's smirk shifted to a grumble. Suddenly, he walked over to PaNou and pushed her to the floor and rushed to grab a bamboo stick. He returned and he began slashing PaNou on her back.

She screamed and dropped to the ground.

"Do you know who gave birth to you? Who fed and raised you!" Blong roared.

"Stop this right now!" Youa stepped in between the two. In the process, she knocked over the large bowl of chicken. The pot clanged and spun to a halt. "Old Man, what are you doing! She's also my daughter, and she is no longer a kid."

"She is my blood. I can do whatever I think is right, and for as long as she still lives in my house, she will respect her father. Did you see her? She yelled in my face! That big mouth of hers, hear my words—one day she'll be in big trouble and no one will care." Blong threw the bamboo stick down and walked away.

Youa wrapped her arms around the much-shaken PaNou. She patted her daughter's head. "PaNou, you shouldn't have done that. Learn to shut your mouth and listen. You know your father has a short temper."

"I've shut my mouth my entire life. Can't I just speak once? Just once?" She sobbed. "I know for sure now he doesn't love me."

"Don't you say that. He does. He just shows it in such a harsh way sometimes."

PaNou tried to get up but fell on one knee. With the help of her mother, she slowly stood on wobbly legs. "He's not my father. My real father would never hit me."

"PaNou, I told you not to say that."

She spun her arm from her mother. Holding her elbows, PaNou dropped and bawled, "Why couldn't he keep fighting in the war. I wish the Vietnamese would kill him!"

"Close that mouth of yours right now! Why does your tongue speak so much fire?"

There was no answer. Only weeping.

"Go to your room right now and sleep. If I hear you speak like that again, I'll whip you, too. No wonder your father is *angry* at you." While Youa walked to the kitchen she yelled, "That Cheng isn't even handsome. I just don't know why you're so crazy for him!"

Weeks passed and the young couple's relationship intensified. After the debacle with her parents, PaNou was doing her best to ensure Cheng visited at the safest of times, which was mostly at dusk. Though Blong and Youa never caught the elusive Cheng, locals confirmed more sightings each passing day.

By now, Blong and Youa realized that no matter how much they told PaNou she wasn't going to listen. With haste, they began searching for a suitor. They proposed to wed her to a wealthy cousin, Kai Thao, who lived in a village to the north. Kai, whom PaNou had met only a few times, was in his late forties, and already had two wives and six kids, two of which were older than PaNou. Despite these pitfalls, Kai was wealthy—even wealthier than Blong.

On an early evening, there was a knocking on the door. PaNou rushed to the door and opened it. A man with round shoulders, thin eyebrows, and a prickly moustache stood, studying her. Up and down. He had lots of visible white strands standing in his shiny black hair. She had seen him before but didn't remember his name.

"Welcome. My dad isn't home right now. He'll—"

"Not a problem."

"My mom's in her room. I'll go get her—"

"No need to." He eyed her. "PaNou, right?"

PaNou leaned her head forward. "Yesss..."

"These past few years, you've grown a lot." Without blinking, he continued, "I'm Kai, Kai Thao, and how are you today?"

Her body iced. "Oh, you are my...cousin, right?"

He locked his eyes on her. Afraid and nervous, PaNou tried her best to remain calm and be polite.

"Bet you don't know I helped your parents name you? It's interesting how things work out."

"Actually, I don't like my name at all." She tried desperately to not make any eye contact. Such new knowledge made her even more uncomfortable. "Well, let me go get my mom—" She turned toward the hall.

"PaNou."

Without answering, she stopped her steps.

"I know you think I'm too old for you—rather, I see it as a good thing..."

PaNou turned away.

"Your parents also see something really good in this. Listen, I'm established. I can take care of you. You will never have to worry about anything."

PaNou answered insipidly, "It's okay because I'm not the type of person that worries too much."

"I want to take the time to love you, PaNou."

"Thank you, but I have already found my love."

Kai reached out a gold ring, spun it a few times, looked out to the road for a brief moment, and fixed his sleeves. "So these stories we hear of this orphan boy, Cheng, is he that special to you? I've seen him before—to be honest, he's quite short and...well, maybe you can tell me, does he ever take a shower? Not to mention he's not handsome one bit. You deserve to be with someone better."

An inferno imploded PaNou's heart. Eyebrows drawn inward, eyes pierced, and lips tightened like zippers, she turned enough so she was looking at Kai from the corner of her eyes.

"He's a hundred times more handsome than you, so what does that make you then?"

111

Head down, Kai nodded and smiled. "Your words are very sharp." He cleared his throat and aimed the gold ring at the ceiling. "I have a very busy schedule today, but I made the effort to come talk to you. I see, I'm clearly wasting my time. To be truthful, you are too immature for my taste. I'm only doing this because I want to help your parents."

PaNou's face tightened.

Kai headed out the door. "You know, I never did marry my true love. I had the chance, but I wasn't such a risk taker like you." He looked into space and nodded, "There are days I think of her. That high-pitched laugh of hers." Kai looked at PaNou. "You believe that there's such a thing as 'True Love'?"

PaNou refrained from responding.

"Of course," Kai grinned. He began walking out the door but stopped for another second. "If you change your mind, please know my heart will always have a place for you. I take good care of my wives. Don't believe me, I beg you to ask them yourself." Kai turned away and walked out. "I look forward to taking care of you."

All PaNou could fathom was rage. Her eyes swelled. She was breathing hard. So hard it hurt. Youa walked out from her room while tying the front of her sash.

"Why do you always look so mad?"

PaNou shook her head in long swoops—her long black hair swirled in slow motion.

"PaNou, did I ever tell you how beautiful—"

"Mom! How could you do this?" PaNou shouted. She grabbed a stool and threw it against the wall. When it didn't accomplish what she wanted, she charged the wall and began tearing out the bamboo splints.

"Has the devil gotten into you?"

PaNou continued ripping.

"Why is your father not here!"

"Mom! I hate you! I hate you and Dad so much!"

"That tongue of yours, I'm going to really have to cut it off."

"I'd rather die than marry that old guy."

"Who are you talking about?"

"Don't try to be dumb! Kai! He was just here."

"He was? Why didn't you come get me?"

"I hope he never comes back."

"PaNou, you need to understand that Cheng must be avoided. And plus, if you marry Kai, you and your future children will have a great life. You wouldn't even have to do anything!"

PaNou grabbed her face in disgust. The last thing on her mind was having kids with Kai. She felt betrayed, especially by her own mother. Burning with rage, she began punching into the bamboo wall. After weakening the wall her right fist broke through the shingles, but the separate splints snatched her wrist as she tried to pull out.

"Why are you so dumb? You should be fortunate both your mom and dad are alive. Because we love you— that's why we're going to make sure you have a good life."

"I'm tired of you and Dad controlling me. Why can't I decide what I want to do with my life for *once*?"

"You are like a blind kid who is walking toward a cliff; if your mother and father didn't care, then we would let you fall off."

PaNou finally yanked her hand out. It was bleeding.

Youa grabbed a small cloth, tore it down the center, and wrapped it over PaNou's wrist.

"Listen, your Cheng will not be able to take care of you. Look at your oldest sister, Ka's life—learn from her." Youa held her daughter's hand. "You were too young to remember when she ran off with Lo. Your father and I warned her many times that Lo's animal spirit did not suit hers. Look now. She used to have a big mouth until Lo punched her teeth out. Now Ka has permanent bruises all over her body. She can't leave either because no man wants her now. Ka's only twenty-six and looks older than me. Do you understand what I'm trying to tell you?"

"Then why don't you and Dad go do something about it?"

"Why don't you understand? Once you marry, you belong to your husband's family."

"That's stupid!"

"No, what's more stupid is if we let you marry Cheng." She felt the side of her daughter's face. "I want to see you with a man who can take care of you."

"Cheng isn't anything like Lo, Mom. He's different. I know he would never have the heart to hit me." PaNou could not help but think, *If he ever did try, I'm bigger than him anyway.*

"Why is your skull so thick? You still don't understand what I'm telling you."

PaNou reminded, "Mom, but didn't you tell me that a flowing river cannot be stopped? I thought you understood me. "

"I do, and I want to guide the river to a better destination." Youa looked PaNou straight in the eyes and held both her hands. "You are my youngest daughter, and I love you. Kai will take really good care of you."

"But Kai's almost as old as Dad. It makes me want to just puke."

Blong happened to be at the front door and interjected, "When you get older, you'll thank us. Say all you want because you have no choice. It's been done. Tomorrow Kai will be here—"

PaNou ran to her room. She could hear her parents talking.

"I saw Kai on the way home. We spoke a bit and everything is a done deal. Fifteen silver bars and four cows."

Youa gasped. "Why didn't you get more?"

"He offered it. So I took it."

A mixture of adrenaline and anger rushed through PaNou's veins. She clamped her wrapped wrist. The pain thudded with sharp zings.

Upset because her parents had controlled her entire life and were going to control her future as well, PaNou finally made up her mind and opted for the plan Cheng had proposed: escape to Tong Shia. Not too long ago it seemed all a crazy idea. Now, the name Tong Shia had the sound of bells ringing from heaven.

The time to execute the getaway was immediate. That night Cheng carefully swooped from shadow to shadow. Little did he realize she was already outside—waiting. As soon as he sat against the wall, PaNou jumped from the corner—snatching his forearm with an iron grip. Cheng shriveled with sudden fear.

"Let's go." She yanked him forward before he could catch his first breath.

Cheng was still shaking from fright but acted like it never occurred. "What did you say?"

"Let's go to Tong Shia."

"Wait." Cheng gave her a stern look. "At one time you said it was a crazy idea."

"This time crazy is good."

Cheng scratched the back of his head.

"Honey," PaNou interrupted, "tomorrow my parents are forcing me to marry this one old man."

"Let's go then."

PaNou planted her feet firmly and looked back to her room.

"What is it?"

"I still need to grab a few things." PaNou rushed inside and gathered a pair of shirts into her cone-shaped bamboo basket. She slid on her green sandals and was outside within minutes.

"Wow, that was quick."

"Here." PaNou tossed a pair of sandals. "I got these for you."

"Thank you! And they're also blue." Cheng quickly switched to his new sandals and tossed his old ones into the forest. "Let's—"

Before Cheng finished his sentence, PaNou snatched his arm.

What a strong grip! Cheng thought.

Led by a small candle, they walked into the darkness.

Before the house disappeared behind the trees, PaNou stopped to look back one last time. A mixture of joy and uncertainty coated her expression. Cheng ran his fingers through her hair and brushed it behind her ears.

"From today on, no looking back. Only forward."

She nodded.

"No matter what happens, I'll be here." Cheng lifted her chin. "I love you."

"I love you, too."

"Are you scared?"

"No," said PaNou, holding on to Cheng's hand firmer, and they increased their pace.

Without further words, the two began the arduous six-hour walk to Tong Shia. Within an hour, the candle began to flicker out. The intermittent wind hustled from the nearby branches with a cold bite. Cheng walked with one palm cupping the front of the candle.

"Why don't you use a new candle?" PaNou leaned closer to Cheng.

"Well, if I knew we were doing this tonight I would've brought more."

"It's too dark. I can't see anything."

It would be another five or more hours before sunrise, and just as long before they would reach Tong Shia. Cheng was baffled on what to do next. There was no way they'd get there without more light.

"Let's go over here." PaNou tugged Cheng by their locked elbows.

They strayed from the narrow path and into the thicker and darker part of the jungle. Trampling over woven roots and bending under low branches, PaNou found a small open ground. The flame was burning with its last effort.

"Well, I guess here will be okay." She scanned the area with large eyes. Some of the hanging branches looked like giant hands reaching over to grab them.

"You want to rest here?"

"Where else can we go?"

"Yeah, you're right," said Cheng.

The multiple sounds of high-pitched croaking, rapid shuddering, and deep eerie sounds amplified. Cheng brushed his side against her.

"Are you scared?"

"No," said Cheng. "But I'm kind of cold." Hastily, he tore a few banana leaves and made a place to sleep on. The two hid under the cover of banana leaves and within seconds, the candled flickered into darkness. Through the cracks of the canopy, the abundance of stars brightened to life. The two gaped above.

"When I was small I used to always wish I'd catch a star. I tried jumping to catch them and when I didn't, I cried and cried. So eventually, I gave up. They're too high to reach." PaNou sighed, "Maybe one day."

"Really? I tried catching them too—I've always wondered how far they really are. But I don't have to anymore because I'm already with the brightest star."

"You and your sweet words." PaNou searched for his hand. When she did, she brought it to her face and gently, she kissed his hand. Then she hugged Cheng's hand against her chest. Cheng wiggled closer until his lips were behind her neck, and gave her a soft "good night" kiss.

Cheng woke up first to a fierce chatter and covered PaNou's mouth. Behind a small group of soldiers walked two Hmong couples, followed by children. They hid quietly under the pile of leaves. Cheng and PaNou couldn't understand the soldiers but could tell from the words they were Vietnamese—likely, the Viet Cong. The soldiers were passing through the jungle, not following the path whatsoever. They passed a few yards behind the massive trunk that blocked their view of Cheng and PaNou. When the sounds grew faint, PaNou stood to look. A little girl with uneven bangs and dirt smeared all over her face was the last one in line. In one hand she held a rag that looked like a doll wrapped in a blanket. She was crying and just as she turned back, she made eye contact with PaNou. Instantly, they disappeared into the forest. Cheng pulled PaNou down.

"What are you doing?" Cheng whispered.

"The little girl, I've seen her before. Oh no, she's the girl from…" PaNou's mouth remained open.

"We better get going." Cheng held her hand and off they went. For the next few hours, they traveled inside the jungle, keeping close to the path.

The air—humid and thick—pasted PaNou's long hair across her face. After seeing the Viet Cong soldiers, they didn't speak much but increased their pace. As they started gaining higher elevation the air cooled and the jungle thinned out.

Puffing, PaNou stopped by a vine-covered tree.

"Let's rest."

"Let's keep going. We're almost there," said Cheng.

PaNou grabbed a low-hanging branch to balance herself. Right away, something slithered on her hand. She screamed, breaking pieces of the branch in the process.

"Snake!"

"Don't make so much noise." Cheng searched the ground covered with dead branches and leaves. "Where is it? I don't see it."

PaNou's eyes scanned intermittently.

"Are you sure it was a snake?"

"I'm sure. It crawled on me." The two looked around each other. Various sizes of broken branches littered the floor, making it difficult to find the serpent.

Startled, the green tree viper swirled quickly by Cheng's side.

"There it is!" PaNou pointed.

Cheng braced himself while PaNou stood against a tree. The snake moved toward PaNou. Instinctively, Cheng took hold of a large branch from the ground, and with it, he hammered the snake. With the head crushed, its body swirled rapidly. The two watched—clinging on to each other.

PaNou ran back to the trail with Cheng in pursuit.

"Let's stay on the trail."

"All right," Cheng said, catching his breath.

They were now more than halfway to Tong Shia, and having gained enough elevation, they could see a few villages below. Ahead of them stood a towering mountaintop swallowed by a large cloud. Cheng breathed with a smile.

"Once we get around that mountain, we'll see the village."

"You've been here before?"

"No, my father told me. Before I was born, he lived in Tong Shia for a few years."

PaNou nodded. Her toes were stuffed with leaves around the thongs of her sandals and she wiggled the leaves off. The two followed the trail upward with PaNou in front.

The sun broke through the sheet of clouds. A cool breeze dried the sweat off Cheng's forehead. The sandals PaNou brought for him were two sizes larger and they clapped twice as loud. After a while, he began dragging them, and by habit he still had his toes locked to the thong. The next half hour was a steep climb—the two huffed and puffed their way up.

Once they reached a flat surface, PaNou stopped. Cheng had fallen back about twenty yards. She watched him drag his large sandals like heavy skis.

"Sorry, I took a guess," PaNou said. "They are too big for you."

"Oh, they're fine."

"I know you must be tired. Let me carry the basket."

"No, no. I got it." Cheng lifted the straps higher.

Since they encountered the green viper, PaNou had carried the same expression—a depressed look. Cheng folded his sleeves to his armpit and was concerned while she stared blindly to the ground.

"How come you look so sad?"

"I do?—I'm not sad." She looked up, smirked with an eye bigger than the other, and forcibly broke a smile. "I'm a little tired."

Two hours later, they made it around the big mountain and on to another taller one. The trees—shorter. The air—windier and colder. They hiked almost to the summit, then around the rift of the mountainside until they sighted brown roofs in the valley below. Although his thighs were screaming with pain, Cheng bounced with celebration.

The edge of the town was visible behind the pillar of a towering peak that watched their every step from thereon. Two other shorter mountains trapped low-lying clouds into the valley. A tiny violet flower with a golden center caught Cheng's attention. He plucked it and held it to PaNou.

"For me?" PaNou returned an open smile, which gave Cheng fresh legs again. "Thanks, Honey."

"It caught my eyes like the first time I saw you."

"Don't say that! You're making me blush."

He held her hand and they continued while PaNou held the flower up toward the sky. Then she snuggled it behind her left ear. Cheng looked at her and noticed her frown again. He made them stop.

"What's bothering you? You don't look happy."

"I am happy," said PaNou. She flapped her sandals forward.

Cheng pulled her back. "Something *is* bothering you." He twirled his tongue inside his mouth. "Hmm, you miss your family. Is that it?"

"No!" PaNou's lips curled. "I'm glad to be out of that place."

"Then what's bothering you?"

PaNou turned away.

"You need to cheer up. This is a brand new beginning for us." Cheng looked to the valley. "Sweetheart, there's our new home."

"I'm, I'm…" PaNou said without looking.

Cheng held her hand. "It'll be all right. The people in Tong Shia are very nice."

Shaking her head, she peered at Cheng. "It's not that." She picked her lips with her fingers and continued, "My mom said that if you ever encounter a snake in your path…you should turn back and make the trip on a new day. It's supposed to be, uh, I guess a bad sign. Never mind."

"You always believe everything they say. If you're asking me, I think we got very lucky. We could've been captured by those soldiers." Cheng held her hand. "Seriously, we were this close to being captured, but we weren't. See, we have good luck on our side."

PaNou nodded, acknowledging such thought. "Why did you have to kill the snake anyway?"

"Because it was going to attack you."

"Maybe it just wanted to get back on to the tree."

"I don't know, but it was after you." Cheng fixed his sleeves. "Let's not talk about it anymore, okay?"

"Okay."

Tong Shia was different from many villages. Aside from its isolated location, it was home to a unique breed of individuals—mostly individuals who were kicked out of their own clans. The reasons ranged from simply being disobedient to thievery. Most Tong Shia residents minded their own business—a perfect fit for the young couple.

There was no wooden sign to welcome them. No front gate—only rows of small houses and fences. The path led directly into the center road of the village. Many of the homes were set up like abandoned boxes on an open road. It was a transient town as shown by many empty houses.

PaNou and Cheng were greeted by a few folks walking out with baskets and farm tools. No one cared to ask why they came because many of them had their own reasons they weren't fond of sharing. PaNou kept smiling at Cheng until he couldn't stand it anymore.

"What?" Cheng asked.

"Look." PaNou aimed her eyes at a little boy who skipped behind his mother. The boy held a tiny hoe in one hand. "He is so adorable."

"Yeah, he is."

As they walked into Tong Shia, they looked at the passing houses that lined the small road. Many of them were in very poor condition—nothing more than a row of small huts, each tied together with whatever pieces of wood or bamboo was available. A large gust of wind could easily knock many of them over as evident by some piles of former homes.

An old couple stood near the center of the road and greeted them.

"Welcome," the man said. "Are you two here to visit or to live?"

"Hello." Cheng shook his hand. "We want to live here, Sir." Cheng nodded at PaNou, confirming that the people in Tong Shia were, indeed, very nice.

"You pick any one that is empty," spoke the elderly lady with cloudy gray eyes. As she spoke, she looked past them. "Don't pick a house with a dead body in it."

"Excuse me, what did you say?" Cheng's face whitened.

"She's an old woman, but don't take her so seriously," the man smiled.

"From today on, Tong Shia is your home." Then the woman stood silent.

"Thank you," replied PaNou.

PaNou picked the one closest to the front entrance that was vacant: the ninth house. The young couple immediately began cleaning and organizing the tiny structure. The dry leaves on the roof were still in good shape. The frame, on the other hand, tilted and rocked with each gust of wind. And so Cheng spent most of the entire day tightening the frame of the house with ropes that he collected from other abandoned houses. Then he placed small boulders around the base of the house, and dug a tiny moat around the house so rain wouldn't run mud across the floor. Finally, Cheng's dream was being realized. After all the crawling to visit PaNou and the verbal wars between clans, the two were now finally together.

"This is going to be great," Cheng celebrated, as he realigned the door hinges.

"This house has a lot of holes." PaNou slumped on a low wooden platform that was their bed. "I don't like this house."

"Well, you chose it, right?"

PaNou spun her head and looked at the dusty interior. "Can we go back and look around?"

With the end of a rope still in his mouth, he stopped tying the door and turned to her. "We're almost done fixing this house. Let's stay here. Most of them are worse than this one."

PaNou didn't like it. For her, it was a dramatic downgrade to what she was used to. On the other hand, for Cheng it wasn't an exceptional upgrade but slightly better than his prior home, especially with PaNou in his life.

Later that day, the old couple who greeted them returned and donated a pair of chickens and pigs.

"Thank you so much. How should I call you?" Cheng got on his knees to pay gratitude.

"You can call me Grandpa Kong and my wife, Grandma Kong. She's the one who wanted to help you two."

"Thank you. Thank you both for your kindness."

"Don't go killing the chickens and the pigs now," said Grandma Kong. She scratched her black beanie hat that had caterpillar-like ripples on it. Silver strands of hair curled on her shoulders.

"Wait, did you say 'don't kill the chickens and the pigs'?" Confused, Cheng looked to PaNou.

"Young man, you kill them and you will have no more." The old woman gave him a harsh look with her silver eyes. "You two are still kids."

Cheng frowned. *What's the point of having chickens if you can't eat them?*

"We'll take good care of them," PaNou said.

"Son, you are lucky to have a wise wife," said Grandma Kong. She grabbed Cheng's hand, opened it, and closed her eyes. With her index finger, she penciled the lines on Cheng's palm. She mumbled a few sounds while Cheng observed with utmost curiosity. "Apart—very dangerous. Stay together and you both will be very wealthy one day."

Cheng flashed the widest smile. It was finally time someone said something nice about them. There was no way he'd disagree with such words. He fell back on his knees,

123

stood, dropped back on his knees, and repeated this many times to thank the lady.

Months after their daring escape, the young couple struggled and marginally got by each day. They faced new survival methods in farming, bartering, and trying to maintain their livestock. Many of these responsibilities Cheng had never had the chance to learn because his father was rarely home to teach him. PaNou, on the other hand, lived a life where she didn't have to worry, particularly when it came to food.

With each new sunrise, life became harder, further testing their commitment. More than half the crop Cheng planted died, and the plants that survived rarely bore fruit. Meanwhile, the livestock they were trying to raise consumed most of their resources. Food was scarce, so Cheng felt that for the short term it was better to get rid of the livestock by eating it. However, PaNou reminded him of Grandma Kong's words, "It'll pay off in the end." and Cheng refrained.

After a few months, the two had lost a lot of weight, particularly Cheng who did most of the work and ate less. The pressure of fending for themselves began to take its toll. As they struggled to have enough to eat, the feeling of being happy together grew distant.

"Maybe we should never have come here."

"You're saying you regret this?" Cheng threw a hand on his hip and one over his head.

"No," PaNou paused. "I hate this place. There's nothing to cook. Nothing to do. Nothing to eat—" She reflected upon the boring times in Lou Sai and such life then was more exciting compared to Tong Shia.

"Why don't you boil the yam?"

"It's the same yam that's been boiled over ten times. There's nothing left in it. It's the same as drinking warm water." PaNou held the front panel of her skirt that had a turquoise border with red embroideries at the center. The once-shiny blue had faded. It used to have a silky feel, but was now scratchy. Her mother made the panel and it was PaNou's favorite.

Cheng squeezed his brows. "I know life's tough right now, but it will get better. It has to. Just wondering, some days can you clean the house when I get back?" Cheng walked to comfort her, but she pushed him back.

"I'm so tired of us arguing all the time."

"We don't argue *all the time!*" Cheng raised his voice.

"See what I mean!"

"Okay. When you feel better, we'll talk." Cheng placed the cracked yam into a small pail of water and began making a fire at the center of the room. "I'll get some chicken from Grandma Kong tomorrow."

She remained silent.

"I won't be begging. She offered it."

Then PaNou stretched her front hair and began combing it with her fingers. She noticed how filthy and dark her toenails were—where dirt and tiny pebbles had made a home. Then she began sobbing.

"Remember, 'No regrets. No looking back.' That's our motto," said Cheng.

"Just leave me alone."

Seeing her shoulders trembling, Cheng felt guilty to see his beautiful wife in such an unhappy state. He sat there—watching the yam brew in the pail. He stood up with both hands over his forehead. Clang! He kicked the bucket across the room. Cheng knelt down and held his big toe as blood began flowing from it.

With time, the struggles aggravated and so did the disagreements. Bombarded with the misery of survival, many times the young couple argued nonstop—bringing up the past and pushing each other's temper buttons.

"Can you help sweep the floor, Sweetheart?"

"I'm stressed," said PaNou. "Can I do it when I feel better?"

"If I waited until I felt better, I would never go to the farm." Cheng, who had a long day at the farm didn't appreciate her response. Sharp rocks, sticks, and other debris had found their way into the house. This was the fourth time in two days that Cheng had asked, and he was growing impatient. Cheng continued, "The floor isn't going to sweep itself. Don't you want a better life than this?"

"Of course, I do."

"This is a little thing that if you could do, it would make my entire day better. After a hard long day at the farm, the last thing I want to deal with is coming home to sweep the floor."

"If it's a little thing, then why are you making it such a big deal?"

"See this?" Cheng took off his left sandal and brought his feet into the air to show three separate cuts, one still had dried blood on it.

She didn't bother to look.

"Are you waiting for me to get another cut?"

"I'll do it tomorrow then."

In disbelief, Cheng shook his head. "Never mind me ever asking. I'll do it because I do it all the time anyways." He grabbed the broom and began sweeping—each sweep, hard and loud. After struggling a long year in Tong Shia, Cheng murmured, "You know, I just can't be doing everything."

"*Everything*?" PaNou shouted. "I massage your dirty feet, wash your clothing, and I sewed you an extra shirt and pants." She stood up and continued, "I *had* a better life than this! I can't take this anymore." She stormed outside.

Cheng paused, momentarily. Then he darted after her. "I'm sorry, Sweetheart. I'm just very frustrated. I mean I did ask you to sweep the floor a few days ago, and you haven't done it."

"Why do you have to be so controlling?"

"Controlling? I was just asking you to help me out." Cheng held her shoulders. "I had a bad day today, all right? After digging and watering on the field in such a hot day like today and then, this other guy at the farm, I forgot his name, but he was giving me an attitude—treated me like I was so stupid I didn't know how to farm." Cheng paused to take a breather. "What's so difficult about killing weeds? He wanted me to pull them out and I told him cutting them was just fine with me."

She pushed his hands away.

"Hey, I'm sorry, okay?"

They slowly went back inside the house.

"Sweetheart, all I'm asking is if you could just use three minutes to sweep the floor, it'd make a whole world's difference."

PaNou reacted with a silence that Cheng never grew accustomed to.

"Are you thinking about Kai, again?" Cheng grabbed the broom and resumed sweeping.

"What! I thought you said, 'never look back.' Why are you bringing up Kai against me? I don't even care about him."

"Why are you ignoring me then?"

"I wasn't. I was listening to you."

"Well, give me a response or something."

"You just don't understand me."

"Don't understand you? You need to help me understand you," Cheng begged. Then he continued sweeping with loud strokes, hoping that she'd notice and take over the sweeping. When she didn't bother to stand up to help him, Cheng became mad. "I can't read through your thick skull."

"Yeah, keep saying that and one day I will be thinking of Kai."

"Okay, okay. I'm sorry."

Arguments occurred more frequently. On most nights, they hugged and reconciled and during the day, they verbally attacked each other again without hesitation. It was an emotional roller coaster followed by threats of separation.

PaNou had begun to miss her family very much but didn't want to appear emotionally weak. *Will they ever come looking for me? Maybe they don't even care if I'm dead.*

Meanwhile, Cheng was growing weary of farming, cooking, and cleaning. He didn't mind performing such labor at the beginning, but now he felt PaNou could be contributing more. For PaNou, she had grown accustomed to Cheng providing for her, and therefore, took offense to his sudden gripes and lashings.

"I need you to help me out more, Sweetheart."

"I am. What more can I do?"

"Can you help with the dishes, please?"

"I've been washing dishes since I was five years old. I'm not going to do them. I hate doing the dishes."

Flabbergasted, Cheng wrinkled his nose. "I don't think there is any person who wakes up in the morning and looks forward to washing the dishes, Sweetheart."

"Oh, because I'm a woman you want me to always do the dishes, clean, and cook."

"No! That's not it." Cheng had to calm down and try to think of the most logical explanation for her. "I do most of the cooking anyway, but all I'm saying is whoever sees it, just wash it. Why do I need to keep asking you to do things? I think, you and I, we should be able to read each other and help each other out."

"Why are you acting like I've never washed the dishes before?"

After the heated exchange, they slept separately, yet it took less than one night sleeping alone before they remembered the hurdles they had overcome and reconciled.

A portion of Tong Shians was a supportive group. The young couple always welcomed visits from neighbors because the conversations allowed them to forget their hardships. Some visitors brought snacks over. These nibbles went a long way because on most days they were the only food Cheng and PaNou had.

The young couple's infamous tale made its way to the heart of distant villages, even Tong Shia. By then the rumors had grown to gigantic proportions. The rumors portrayed Cheng as a thief and a two-faced man born with bad luck—not to be trusted. PaNou did not fare better. Rumors described her as dumb, lazy, and deceitful, saying she despised her parents and took advantage of them. When people heard about the young couple's reputation, many were less inclined to help. Gradually, neighbors began to avoid the couple. Fewer and fewer visits occurred.

Cheng, who had been establishing himself as a potential leader in Tong Shia was now shunned. When Cheng invited neighbors and friends over no one showed up. Some were disgraced that they had associated themselves with the couple. Viewed as a bad omen, many avoided Cheng and PaNou. In a small place like Tong Shia, it was tormenting.

Cheng ran to his next-door neighbor, Meng, also his closest friend. If there were someone left who would still talk to him, it'd be Meng.

Meng opened the door. Halfway.

"Hey, Meng," Cheng said, leaning his entire hope against the door.

Meng stuck his head out, displaying a big hairy mole on the corner of his cheek.

"Hey, Meng, I need to talk to you."

"It's not a good time to talk."

"Why are you acting like someone's going to shoot you?" Cheng tried to go in, but Meng held the door firm.

"No. No. You see, no one saw this coming except you," said Meng, spinning the extended hair on his mole.

"You're not talking about those stupid rumors?"

There was silence from Meng.

"Meng, I have no control over what people say or don't say—they're not true."

"Don't matter. It's still bad."

"What? You don't believe me?"

"It doesn't matter if it's true or not. It's going around and I don't want a piece of it. I've seen enough troubles in my thirty years. Even in this town."

"But you know me more than anyone else in this town. How can you believe—"

"Look, I don't believe those rumors," said Meng. "Why don't we all take a break from this? It'll be good for you and me. Whenever I'm ready to talk, I'll come over."

"All right, Meng. Have it your way."

"Don't get mad at me. I just don't want people thinking I'm a part of this. That's all."

"But Meng, people respect you. They'll listen to you. I need you to explain to them, that—"

"That's why I can't do this. If I do get involved, people will no longer respect me. We both know it's hard to grow a cucumber but killing it is easy."

Cheng began pacing back and forth.

"Listen. We're still friends. Maybe when the war is over people will forget about all these things." Meng pushed the door against Cheng, and looked away. "Don't take this the wrong way, but I'd appreciate it if you stopped coming over."

Cheng growled, "Next time you need help, you better not be asking me."

Meng slammed the door shut.

Cheng shouted, "You say you want people to respect you, you've lost mine!"

Meng's rejection added to the shockwave of melancholy. Furthermore, Cheng began a habit of ignoring PaNou. When they spoke, he raised his voice. Though unaware of it, he was putting his own frustration on her. Fights erupted. The passing nights grew exceedingly colder.

"We need to get out of this place." Cheng stared into space.

"What happened to 'No regrets. No looking back.'?"

Cheng punched the wall and the house wobbled.

"We can't always keep running. Do you realize what people are going to say about us if we just left?"

"This time, it'll be a place for only you and me. We can start our own village."

"No," PaNou said, shaking her head. Her eyes glimmered. "We're going to stay right here and show them that those rumors aren't true." PaNou sat upright. "Who cares what anyone says? In our hearts, we know we love our families." She looked over to the basket her mom made and took a long breath.

"I'm so tired of this nonsense."

"Honey." PaNou walked to Cheng and grabbed his hand. "People will call us thieves all they want. We know the truth." PaNou began to sob. It was apparent she was giving every ounce of effort to stay strong, but her strength was evaporating. "We'll fight through this together, right?"

"We will." Cheng kissed her on the cheek, held her soft hands, and began caressing them. "You know, though we don't have much, we've helped a lot of people in this village. I'm *pissed* because those bastards act like we're a walking disease or something." Realizing the weakened nature of his wife, he held his emotions together. "I didn't want to tell you this, but two days ago I was over at Meng's house and he said for us to not talk anymore."

PaNou hugged her husband closer.

"Remember, before all this happened he was calling me over almost every single day. I helped him put his table together. Next time he needs help, he better apologize to me first." Cheng walked to the door, looking left to Meng's house. "What can a handicap like him do anyway? He can't do anything with that one leg...he deserved it."

"You shouldn't speak words like that." Suddenly, PaNou heard her mom's voice who used to tell her the same thing.

"I certainly don't feel sorry for him anymore."

Cheng was hurt. Meng had been one of the first individuals to welcome them to Tong Shia. The two clicked immediately and became such good pals that Meng gave one of his dogs named, Chance, to Cheng. Unfortunately, the dog had grown up under Meng's care and for most of the time, resided in its former owner's yard.

After gathering herself, PaNou's eyes began to glitter with hope. "We've gone through worse. We'll overcome this. The more bad things people say about us, the more we must love each other. Just wait—when our life gets better, everyone will want to know us."

"Yeah, you're right," Cheng said. He walked out the door, scouting the neighbors. "When we have money, everyone will want to know us." Cheng rubbed his chin. "I won't forget the faces of those bastards."

The following day, eleven Hmong men dressed in dark green camouflaged uniforms marched into town. Each one had strapped over his shoulder an M-14 rifle. Such visits from soldiers were rare. They brought news of the atrocious war in the jungle.

"My name is Lee Fong Yang." He reached out his right hand, waving it. "My Hmong brothers, right now the Americans are in great need for our help. We, *Hmong,* also need their help." He was the only one of the group wearing a green cap that displayed the word: ARMY. Other villagers soon joined the small crowd that gathered around the soldiers. He continued, "The Americans promised us that if we help them win this war, we'll have our own land here. They also promised that if we lose, they'll take care of us. Right now is the time for us Hmong to unite."

"Americans? I don't trust them. After the war, they'll fly back to their country and leave us to die!" A man shouted and looked back to his co-villagers for support.

"The Americans, they already made an agreement with General Vang Pao." Lee Fong eyed the crowd. "Right now while we're talking, our Hmong brothers are out there fighting in the jungle, dying out there for you, me, for all of us. They are fighting for our future—what about all of you? I want to know, will you fight for your people? For your country? For freedom?"

There was chattering among the villagers.

"You can talk all you want here, but when the Communist soldiers come, as long as you are Hmong they'll not spare any of you."

"I hear that white people eat humans," shouted a villager, and the crowd gasped in horror.

"No, they don't," laughed Lee Fong. "Why would they? Do you know that in America they have stores and food everywhere?" Lee Fong debated with a few men until he began handing out small shiny plastic bags of potato chips. "Here, there's enough for everyone here. If you come with us, you will also get paid more money than what ten of you make in one year combined."

The villagers quieted down.

"Or, like I said, you all can stay here if you want. Eventually, the Communist soldiers will come through this land and kill every one of you. We Hmong don't have another choice."

As if the war followed the soldiers to Tong Shia, on their visit multiple planes shrieked and boomed overhead. Five bombs exploded a few miles south in the lower jungle. The grim reality of war was hitting closer to home than before.

The soldiers were there to recruit, and rested for a few days. With each passing day, more gunfire and bombings occurred. After much fear, the folks in Tong Shia settled down and carried on their lives—living with the biting bullets and ground-shaking bombs.

The eleven soldiers separated, going door to door to find recruits while handing out shiny bags. In a few hours, the initial eleven had grown to over thirty men and boys, who continued knocking on more houses.

Dung! Dung! Dung! The knocks rattled Cheng's thin door.

"All right! I'm coming. What do you want, Meng?" Cheng yelled, and opened the door to see a tall middle-aged man in uniform.

"Do you love your people?"

This guy must be smoking opium! Cheng thought, and stared fiercely at the soldier's bloodshot eyes. They scared him enough that he stared away. "You must be crazy," said Cheng. He wasn't in the best mood for jokes. "Is there something I can help you with?"

"Do you think this is funny?"

"No, why, do you?" Cheng frowned. "Who are you?"

"I'm Sergeant Lee Fong Yang. There is a war happening right now."

"Oh, never noticed. Thought the stars were falling from the skies," Cheng said, cynically.

"If we help the Americans win this war, they promised we'll have our country." His posture was robotic, and he spoke like a ventriloquist.

"This *is* our country."

"No, this land belongs to Laos. The Thai, they have Thailand. Vietnamese, they have Vietnam. We Hmong, we have no land yet."

Cheng was finding it hard to believe him.

Then a bomb screeched from the sky, followed by a massive rumbling and an explosion a few miles away. Everyone turned to look at where the explosion was except the Sergeant. Eyes affixed on Cheng.

"Listen, son. We are now the enemy of the Pathet Lao and Viet Cong. Your Hmong brothers are already fighting out there. Many of us will die, but I want to ask you, will you fight for your freedom?"

"I don't know what you're talking about." Cheng reached for the door.

Sensing the urgency of losing Cheng's interest, he extended his arm to hold the door from being slammed in his face. "You'll be paid with lots of money, if you help."

Cheng released the door and inched closer.

"But more important than money, this war is for our people's future."

"How much money?" Cheng asked, lured by the opportunity to better his life.

"You will have more money than you can ever dream of."

Cheng gave him a heavy stare.

The soldier noticed the young man's deep eye sockets. "Son, keep this." He reached in his pocket and revealed a crisp American twenty-dollar bill, and planted it in Cheng's hands.

Cheng's eyes widened like a child receiving a toy.

"If you stay here, you'll be doing the same thing over and over while your Hmong brothers are out there fighting. This is an opportunity to change your life—and also the lives of our people." Lee Fong grabbed Cheng's fingers and folded them over the twenty-dollar bill.

Cheng's eyes widened.

The commotion caught the attention of PaNou who walked in from the back. Lee Fong glanced over Cheng's shoulder and saw a scarecrow-like woman weaving nearer.

"With money, you can buy your lovely wife anything she desires."

"Honey, what does he want?" PaNou asked with a hollow voice.

"Oh, nothing. Just you know, stupid men talk," Cheng reassured his wife. "Why don't you go and make some rice, Sweetheart?"

"We're completely out. Maybe you can go ask Meng again?"

Cheng's face shrunk at the thought of Meng.

The soldier realigned his cap, then placed a hand on the young man's shoulder. "Think about it. We'll come back another time. You have until then to decide." The Sergeant walked directly to the next house.

Normally, the recruiting officer would've given up on the first try, but they needed every man. The Americans had suffered major casualties. The offer made to the Hmong was too great for General Vang Pao to ignore—the promise of a brighter future, which included freedom, money, and education was far better than a hostile environment many Hmong felt would be their fate in Laos. Winning the war would bring the ultimate gift to the Hmong people: sovereignty.

Fighting for his people was important, but above all else, finding the quickest route to improve their life preoccupied Cheng. The sound of money sung beautifully. He was simply tired of being poor—tired of being hungry, detesting every second of it. Ever desperate, Cheng was willing to find any means to make money, to have a better life with PaNou. And, like the story he told PaNou about Tou Cha and the Dragon, Cheng could visualize his pockets overflowing with gold coins.

Each time he saw hunger in his wife's cavernous eyes, it scorched his heart. Her once-sexy curves had eroded to the cliffs of her bones. It was excruciating to witness PaNou withering away. The shadows deepened her cheeks and collarbone. The only features that seemed to grow were her joints—enlarged elbows and knees. The shame took a toll on Cheng. After all, his words, "I'll take care of you." slowly ate away his dignity—no longer could he bear to look at his wife.

On many occasions, the little food Cheng prepared for her, she instead saved for him. When Cheng asked if PaNou had eaten what he cooked, she would always claim that she was full. PaNou's sacrifice became evident with her shrinking frame.

Each new day exerted more self-blame for Cheng to bear. Finally, Cheng came to his own terms: He would sacrifice anything to better their life. The news that Americans needed more Hmong soldiers couldn't have arrived at a better time.

When Cheng approached PaNou about the proposition of enlisting, she became inflamed with rage.

"You told me! You told me you would never leave me. How could you—"

"I'm not leaving you." Cheng ran his hands over her head. "Sweetheart, I'll only be away for some time. But I'll return, I promise."

"You can't go...no, you can't, Honey." She dropped on her knees and tied her arms around him. "I won't let you."

"I have to, so I can take better care of us, and take care of you."

"No, you can't go. What if you don't come back?"

"Sweetheart, I will come back."

"They'll kill you like everyone else."

"I will be most careful. You have my word." Cheng comforted her boney fingers. "Listen to me. I will return for you. Don't you worry so much, okay? When I was speaking with that one soldier, he told me that many of us will return home." Cheng lied for he knew nothing of war. The recruiting officer also made no such comment.

For three straight days, they argued and fought about the subject of Cheng leaving. Once again, they slept separately—one on the covered wooden bed and the other on the blanketed floor.

The passing nights alone grew more frigid. Whenever Cheng tried to speak to her, she'd cover her ears. On the third night, Cheng desperately wanted to break the silence and so he pulled her hands away from her ears.

"I will send you a lot of money—for food, clothing, and I can get that knife I've always wanted. Think about it, we'll never have to starve *ever* again."

PaNou covered her face toward the floor.

"Sweetheart, why don't you understand?—"

"It's two years!"

"I know it sounds long. But the sun rises and sets quickly. Before we know it, two years will pass. I'll write you often and send you money—"

"Money's not going to buy your life back." PaNou spoke with soggy eyes. She shivered. Her sobbing resonated in the room.

Cheng hunched, and looked away.

Weeks passed and the same Hmong soldiers returned. For Cheng, the wait was too long. The soldiers were to spend one night and leave with new recruits early the following morning.

Over half of the remaining men and boys in Tong Shia joined. For many of them, their service would be indefinite.

The night the armed men arrived, Cheng grew restless. At one point when PaNou had cried her eyeballs dry, in order to calm her, Cheng compromised and agreed not to go. Yet, poverty burned him and the vision of money lured him once again.

After the rooster's first crow, two rows of soldiers began forming outside. Cheng hadn't slept all night. As the two lines of men were marching out, he sat upright in the kitchen, gazing at the passing shadows. The weeklong layer of crumbs and dust on their dining table caught his attention. It reopened the grim reality of their struggling life, and reinforced Cheng's decision to enlist. He knew the risk; it would be the furthest and longest that they would be apart.

Cheng found PaNou sitting on the end of their bed staring into space. He cleared his throat a few times to grab her attention. He battled enough courage and walked to her.

"Hi, Sweetheart—"

"You're going, aren't you?" PaNou sat forward with her elbows on her thighs and her head parallel to the floor. Her long hair curtained her disheartened face. "You, you never listen to me."

"Never? You have to stop using that word." Cheng took a deep breath. "I know it'll be tough, but it'll be worth it." Cheng tried to smile, and blinked rapidly.

Her heart sank. She knew there was nothing else she could do to change Cheng's decision.

"I'm sorry…you'll have to forgive me."

"How could you even think about leaving me?"

"Sweetheart, this will be the first time and last time that I won't listen to you. I'm going."

"No, there's no way I'm letting you go." She clutched his forearm.

Cheng took a deep breath and looked away. His eyes sunk low. "I already gave him my word. That's why he gave me money."

She pulled Cheng's entire arm to her. "No, no. You're not going. I won't let you."

"I'm doing this for us. When I come back, we won't have to struggle like this anymore. Plus, I won't have to ask you to do the dishes or sweep the floor again. In fact, you won't have to do anything at all."

"Why are you *always* using those against me?"

"Always?" Cheng swayed his head, then narrowed his lips and brows. "I'm going." He stared out the door, at the line of Hmong men. He didn't want to be harsh, for he knew he'd hurt her, but Cheng felt it was the only way. "Stop controlling me."

PaNou looked up. Shocked. Numbed. Slowly, she released her grip and looked away. "Fine. I won't control you anymore."

"I'll send you money and I'll write you every day."

She had no choice but to accept Cheng's rationale. No matter what happened, PaNou wanted to hear one more time from her husband's own lips that he would return.

"I need you to be strong, Sweetheart," said Cheng. "We've gone through some tough times, but you must believe that we'll be able to overcome this also."

"I will miss you too much."

"I will miss you, too."

"Then you must give me your word that you will return."

"Of course, I will and our life will be so much better. I can't wait until I slap that money in Meng's face." Comforting her, Cheng reaffirmed, "Sweetheart, look at me. I *will* return for you."

"I don't believe you." She walked away and leaned against the wall by the wooden bed, swaying her head. The sparkle of her black hair had dulled quickly in Tong Shia. Her long hair draped all over her face and thin body.

Cheng made slow steps to the door.

"Before you leave, you must raise your hand to the Sky," she demanded, for the Sky was like God to the Hmong. It would serve as both witness and deliverer.

Cheng's eyebrows jumped. He was shocked at her sudden approval because he was still expecting another verbal carnage. Staring at her vertical arm, Cheng joyfully smiled—then pointed his hand to the ceiling.

"First thing I'll do when I get back is buy you that white dress you've always wanted."

"I don't care about the white dress. No matter what happens, I'll wait here for you."

PaNou reached under the bed. She handed over a small pack of food wrapped in dark green banana leaves.

"No, I'll be fine." He pushed the bundle back.

"I won't forgive you if you don't take this."

Cheng nodded. "Take good care of yourself, Sweetheart." He pulled her hair back and kissed her on the forehead.

She couldn't find the strength to look him in the eyes.

He turned to the door, and PaNou pulled him back. Without further words she pressed her head on his shoulder and wailed—the loudest and heaviest tears she'd ever shed. Cheng gently caressed her head.

"Be strong. No matter what happens, I will return." Those were the last words from Cheng.

The two lines of Hmong soldiers were passing their house. Cheng pried PaNou off as carefully as possible and rushed out the door to the end of the line. Sergeant Lee Fong trailed behind the marching men, yelling out orders. He turned and waved at Cheng.

"Hustle now!" shouted the Sergeant.

Cheng paused briefly, turned around, and gave PaNou a slight smile, signaling that he loved her. In seconds, he was camouflaged within the green mass of freedom fighters.

Cheng dipped his head low to hide his tears from the other men. He was the last in line.

PaNou fought her way to the door, almost falling flat as if all her joints had melted. She grabbed the side of the door for support—watching as the men and boys passed up, over, and behind the mountainside. The wind blew a trail of brown dirt behind the soldiers. When the shoulders and heads of the last soldiers disappeared over the high ground, PaNou found herself standing taller to absorb the last second of Cheng. She saw his head spin around to look back, but it was a second too late. He was gone behind the hills. Like the monsoon, tears gushed endlessly down her cheeks—dripping off her chin. PaNou didn't care to wipe.

She stood by the entrance—for a long time. When wind-blown dirt began collecting on her cracked cheeks, she turned to the house. After a lengthy look at the inside of their home—it had never felt so empty—just four walls and a roof. Alone.

A few hours later, Cheng's departure painfully began to digest. The plate where he had eaten the previous night sat at the end of the uneven table. PaNou sat on their bed and pretended to watch Cheng eat like she used to. Then she walked to the table. There, she picked up the spoon Cheng had last used. Eyes closed, she clasped it. The warmth of her husband's hand around the utensil never felt so absent. There were a few hardened rice grains that Cheng had missed on the table. She placed them in her mouth until her saliva softened them as much as possible before crunching them.

Eyes shut, and holding the spoon as steady as possible, she tasted it and whispered, "Honey, do you know that I miss you so much already? Can you hear me?"

Only the rustling of the roof answered back.

Somewhere in the house, Cheng's presence was still warm. It was surreal. For the time being, all she could do was think of him—wishing that he'd be back in a minute. Each passing hour pressed her head lower.

Cheng's scarlet sash on his bamboo stool caught her attention. PaNou walked to it and a comforting sensation lifted her heart. With the sash in her palm, PaNou buried her face in it and sniffed it. The smell wasn't the best—a scent of old dry dirt, but it was the scent of Cheng, only Cheng. She kissed it. Then hugged it against her chest. PaNou untied her green sash and replaced it with Cheng's.

Long days passed. PaNou began to notice the little things that brought memories of her devoted husband. From Cheng's shirts to his farm tools, she knew life alone the next two years would be difficult, but never had she thought it'd be this overwhelming. Fresh imprints of Cheng's bare feet were scattered on the dirt floor. PaNou searched like a spotlight until she found the most defined wrinkles of his feet. Then she found a pair that sat half a yard from the door. She took off her sandals, rubbed out the left footprint of her husband's and made an imprint of her own left foot next to Cheng's. She knelt down and drew a heart around it.

"Honey, wherever you may travel, my love will walk with you also." She wiped her tears and sat down on her husband's stool. "I'm very proud of you—and I can't wait until I see you again."

The agonizing days turned to grueling weeks. The first few weeks were the toughest while PaNou sat inside waiting—waiting for when Cheng normally would return from the farm. But he didn't. Months tumbled by. Sleeping alone had never felt so cold—so frightening. Some nights PaNou would wake up catching herself talking to Cheng.

On one particular night, PaNou had a vivid dream: She was ill and was crying on the bed alone, meanwhile, a thunderous downpour outside shook the house. Then the door opened, and in walked Cheng with his military shirt and black pants. Cheng never matched the military persona, but rather, he looked comical wearing such uniform. Though it was raining very hard, he was as dry as sand. He came to bed, lifted her, and hugged her.

"Sweetheart, the only time I ever want to see you cry again is when you're happy, you hear?"

PaNou hugged him tightly—never to let go.

"I told you I was coming back." He pointed outside. "Hey, look what I brought you."

In walked a snow-white horse with golden hooves beaming a blinding white light.

"What's that?" PaNou opened her sticky eyelids.

"This is a magic horse, and it can take us anywhere we want to go."

Suddenly, PaNou's ailment vanished. "Can it make any wish come true?"

"*Anything* you want. Even to catch the stars, like you've always wanted."

PaNou paused for a second, looking weary. "I don't want to catch the stars anymore."

"Why not?" Cheng asked, looking disappointed. "But you've always said—"

"I want to be with you," she said, softly. "Hold me, please."

"Hey, hey there. C'mon, you know I'll always be here for you." Cheng clasped his hands behind her back. Then he gently kissed her on the lips.

PaNou woke up—scanning frantically around the house. She discovered her own arms wrapped around herself. Cold. Alone. Yet, she felt the pressure on her lips—the soft sweet taste of his lips. PaNou curled under the thin blanket in a fetal position and whimpered like a puppy. She closed her eyes again, wishing to fall asleep to continue the dream. That night she cried her soul dry.

A year passed and there was no news from her husband. PaNou had become little of her former self—a cocoon, simply waiting for life to return. When the remaining ounce of hope began to diminish, a small package enclosed with a note finally arrived. PaNou opened the letter so fast she almost tore it to pieces. Inside, the package was stuffed with enough cash to last years. She jumped and danced around with an immense thrill—not for the money, but to know that Cheng was alive and well.

With the letter in her hand, she waved it with joy. The words were written with haste, skipping across the corners and edges of the paper. The message was short and direct:

Sweetheart,

This war is far from over. I don't know exactly when, but I will be back home as soon as possible. I miss you very much.

Love Forever,

Cheng

PaNou dug inside the packet to see if there was another note. She turned it upside-down, shaking it several times to be certain. There wasn't. She looked behind the light brown paper for other words—no, nothing else. She read the words over and over a thousand times. With the letter in her grip, she couldn't help but think, *My Honey was holding this paper when he wrote.* That night PaNou slept with the letter hugged to her lips.

PaNou waited by the door everyday, looking out toward the dirt road—hoping for that familiar figure to appear.

Words soon spread through many villages that a beautiful woman was living by herself while her husband had yet to return from war. The situation attracted a mob of both single and married men from nearby and distant villages. These men knew the odds: For all the men who left their wives and families to go to war, only a few returned. It wasn't long before a throng of such men courted PaNou and flooded her front door.

PaNou was more prized than other women. Though she had thinned greatly, she was still stunning, young, and she had no children. The men sought to win her heart by convincing her that Cheng was either dead or he had found another woman.

With her faith in the Sky, she maintained her vow. The traffic of incoming and outgoing men trampled all over Cheng's footprints, including the one she had marked and tried to save. The men's efforts were futile. Half a year passed and many men gave up. When they left, their masculine presence made her missed Cheng severely. She yearned for his voice, touch, and large golden-brown eyes. PaNou's faith in the Sky remained strong. The men's one-trick ponies did not tarnish the surface of her loyalty, rather they made her missed Cheng even more.

PaNou kept all her senses alert for any sign of Cheng. Despite reports that many men had been killed, she maintained high aspirations and was thrilled to save as much of the money Cheng sent as possible to surprise him.

Many months passed. No letter. Her heart thickened with a layer of dread. Soon, she fell into a dark rift believing that perhaps, Cheng was dead. Her nightmares became regular episodes. How would she know? If he were killed who would tell her if? The thoughts haunted her more than hunger.

About every other month, at least two corpses were carried into the village. On every occurrence, she rushed to identify them, but only witnessed war's dark consequences. Some unfortunate bodies suffered such horrific explosions that they were unidentifiable. The flesh on some of the faces had melted and dried so quickly together it formed uneven contours and scars. Other bodies were charred entirely. PaNou could only pray that none was Cheng.

After viewing corpses for many months, PaNou could no longer tolerate the inspections. The bodies seemed to arrive in worse condition each time. Finally, she went over and asked Cheng's one-legged friend, Meng, to do the task, compensation included.

"Please, Meng, I—"

"That's fine. You're going through a lot. I'll check them for you," Meng murmured.

"I know you two didn't talk much after those stupid rumors—"

"Forget about what happened." He looked up at PaNou and acknowledged, "Like you say, they're stupid rumors. No matter. I know he's a good person, and to me, we'll always be friends."

"Thank you, Meng." PaNou reached her hand forward. "Here."

"Don't do that," Meng said, shaking his head. He began to walk away, balancing on a wide stick. "You and Cheng have helped me a lot. Besides, I've been checking them anyway."

PaNou followed Meng and he stopped. "Please. I know it's not much but take this money. It'll make me feel better."

Meng stepped back.

"Please…"

Quietly, Meng snagged the dollars. "You know, you don't have to—"

"I know," PaNou said, observing the sky.

"I've never seen any couple love each other as much as you and Cheng." Meng said with saddened eyes. "Keep your head up. I know he'll return. Just a feeling."

PaNou returned a smile, realizing her lips hadn't stretched that far apart since Cheng was around. It took effort.

"It must be difficult for you."

"Sometimes I wonder if death is better."

"No. Don't say that. Don't invite death." Meng snatched the front of his own shirt, pulling it. "Trust me. Death surrounds us wherever we go, so please don't invite it."

"I don't know what's happening to me," said PaNou. With her eyes, she implored Meng for sympathy.

Meng looked her up and down. "How are you getting by?"

"I eat enough to stay alive. Sometimes Grandma Kong comes over to visit or bring food." PaNou sighed, "I don't know if I can keep going like this."

"I hate war." Meng looked over to the unclaimed corpses by the road. "Let me tell you something. In war, there is no winner." He began digging with his cane. "Cheng is going through something harder than we both can even imagine. I'm praying for the best for you two. I know there isn't a single minute that passes that he isn't thinking of you."

"I don't know, Meng. I...I've been having some bad dreams lately." PaNou glanced at the murky mountains.

Meng's ears propped back and his head tilted forward.

"I was running through the woods into this open field of grass. There was this very loud caw..." PaNou's eyes fluttered as she spoke. "Louder and louder the cawing came after me. Then from the sky, what looked like a black cloud was a giant raven swooping down directly at me. Then it snatched me by the arms." PaNou grabbed her bicep to demonstrate. "It carried me high above into a cave on a mountainside. The raven's cawing changed into this witch's laughter that came from the dark sky." PaNou noticed an enlarging dark cloud behind Meng while she spoke. "The witch's laughter came closer and closer into the cave—that's when I woke up—"

"You must be kidding," said Meng, catching his breath.

"No, I'm not. The scariest part was when I woke up, I could still hear the witch's voice—fading into the corner of the house."

Meng's face whitened as if he had seen a ghost and gasped, "This is bizarre, but I had almost the same dream last night. A raven attacked me also and when I killed it, it turned into a monstrous creature. I then regretted killing it because the monster chased me into..." Meng paused. "Into a cave high in the mountains."

PaNou whispered the last few words "into a cave high in the mountains" at the same time as Meng.

"Mine was last night too," PaNou's jaw quivered.

"That's...I don't know what to make of it." Meng shook his head. "Oh, forget it. They're just dreams. It hasn't been easy for all of us. My oldest son, Lue—he left with them too."

147

"Lue. But he's only thirteen?"

"No, eleven. He didn't tell me or his mother. Maybe I should've never said those things to him." Meng hid his face from breaking down and began walking toward a corpse that had just arrived.

PaNou's shoulders dropped. She watched Meng lean against his stick while he inspected. Meng was silent for a few minutes, and suddenly, he broke out a cry. If PaNou wasn't there, she would've mistaken the cry for a child's.

"Oh, Bee. Why did you have to come home like this! Why?" Meng recognized a string necklace. Bee was a close friend of Meng's.

Speechless, PaNou walked back to her dark house that appeared more and more like the cave in her dream.

The incoming corpses carried with them an aroma of death that drenched Tong Shia. It tainted PaNou's hope. The melancholy left its markings. Craters lined her once-beautiful eyes and mapped across her forehead. She became increasingly fidgety.

Later, there was a knock on the door. It wasn't Cheng. Cheng would have just pushed it open. Not in a good mood, she opened the door without asking.

"Meng?"

"Can I come in?"

PaNou had no reaction. She knew Meng, but she didn't like having any man inside the house. She knew Cheng wouldn't have allowed it.

Meng walked inside with his cane. PaNou was still at the door.

"This war, it's really going to get worse."

PaNou nodded. "I hope Cheng is okay. *This* is killing me. I knew I would miss him very much, but never ever like this. I should've stopped him from going."

"Stay strong. I spoke to him sometime before he left. Cheng is very stubborn. He was going to go, no matter what anyone said. That stubbornness might come back against him...I don't know. To be honest, if I were him, I would've never left my wife alone."

148

"Something tells me he'll return." PaNou looked out the door. "Would you wait for your love even if it was ten years?"

"No. Not even one year. You?"

"For the love of my life...hmmm, yes, if it was guaranteed he would return."

"But what if he did something bad?"

"What do you mean?" She frowned.

"Let's say, what if he was with another woman, would you still love him?"

"He wouldn't do that. I know he loves me too much to hurt me."

"To be frank, I'm a man, and I certainly don't want to disappoint you but no matter how strong love is, a man needs...how should I say this, yes, the touch of a woman. You see..." Meng gave her a probing look, "there is no touch like a woman's touch. Every woman has this..." Meng was waving his hands to find the word, "this gift."

PaNou turned away. "He's different. I know he wouldn't. He's not that type of person. Besides, I don't think there are any women soldiers in the war."

"No, but he'll see plenty in villages that they stay in, or that they pass through. Now, keep in mind that many of these women too are alone. Their husbands have either been killed or left to war. It's bound to happen—even to the most loving husband, or wife, for that matter." Meng came closer to PaNou, and she backpedaled. "I've *seen* it."

Her instincts came back. "You were a soldier for a year, right?"

"Ten months—until I got my leg blown up. Gosh, I should have let someone else lead first."

"So did you...um," PaNou paused to think of the right words, "were you with another woman?"

Meng swallowed. "Well, you see, other men were worse. And at first I felt terrible about it—"

"How could you do that to your wife? She loves you so much. And she was home every day taking care of your kids, cleaning the house, and tending the farm."

"That's because—"

PaNou slapped him in the face. It was an immediate reaction.

Meng released a loud sigh and composed himself. "I was kind enough to come here and was going to offer you a place at my house. But, I'll let you suffer the way you want." Meng tapped his way out the door. "Oh, you know Vong, my youngest son, right?"

PaNou nodded, body pressed against the door. She was ready to kick the cane away if Meng made any further advances.

"I just learned...he's not my son."

PaNou's jaw dropped.

Gone So Long

On an overcast afternoon, a young boy came screaming into the village. Unlike many visitors who came in quietly, the teenage boy ran in yelling, crying, and tripping over himself like he possessed twisted legs.

"What happened?" A villager rushed to the boy's aid. A line of blood sprinkled behind the boy.

"They're all dead! All of them—dead!" the boy bawled. "The jungle, it came alive and killed all of them."

"What happened!" the man asked again.

The boy's chin fell to his chest. Face white as ghost, he struggled, "Th-they're all dead. All dead."

The man looked to the sky—not for help, but in acceptance of The End. A low-flying plane zipped over them and dropped multiple explosives a few miles north. The man comforted the young boy. He wiped the heavy dust from the boy's face.

"Lue," recognized the man.

No response.

"Get Meng here!"

The boy's eyelids flashed and spun to the ceiling—followed by slow and empty puffs. The man lifted the boy's bloody arm from his belly. It revealed a clean cut about six inches across the lower abdomen. A piece of bombshell had sliced open the boy's belly, exposing his tangled intestines.

"Lue!" Meng hopped faster than most men with two legs. He slammed his cane and dove to the ground. "My son, your daddy is here. Daddy is right here." He lightly shook the boy. There was low breathing—each one after, softer and quieter. "My son, why did you leave and not tell your father? Why did you do that!" He hugged Lue's head to his chest.

Lue's mother and other folks rushed in.

PaNou heard the boy's cry, but it didn't sink into her near-mummified mentality. When the neighbors started shouting, their wailing voices finally moved her.

151

"Lue..." PaNou whispered. Then she called, "Cheng."

A small crowd gathered around the boy. PaNou dug herself inside the group. As soon as she clawed into the center, Lue opened his eyes—halfway. They made eye contact. Then he started trembling with quiet whimpers.

"They're all dead," whispered Lue.

"What did you say?" PaNou asked.

Neither Meng nor anyone else answered. Streaks of dark blood stained the boy's skin. His face was a dead yellow. The distasteful smell of human death stained him. A fresh gash serpentined the boy's left thigh. The blood had nearly dried itself out but still revealed desiccated peach-colored fat, which had pumped its way out of the boy's thigh.

"My son, where's everyone else?" Meng asked.

"Th-they're all dead. Everyone with me...all dead....last night we rested...in Lou Sai...all the houses on fire."

"No. No!" PaNou shook her head violently. "That's not true—you don't know. You're just a kid." PaNou knelt in front of Lue. "You don't know where Lou Sai is, right? Tell me."

The boy didn't answer. He grew weaker by the second. His head flopped back into Meng's arm.

"My son!" Meng shook him.

Mom! PaNou's heart cried. The pain was numbing. "No, no, no—it's not true what he's saying!"

"Stop yelling so loud," Meng barked back. "Maybe your Cheng's already dead."

The thought of Cheng overcame her. She shook the boy's shoulders, commanding him, "D-did you see Cheng?"

Lue moved again, slightly, and closed his eyes. Then he coiled his body into a ball. "I-I'm very cold."

PaNou persisted, "Tell me, did you see Cheng?"

Meng looked with unpleasant eyes at PaNou, then back to his fading son. Face swollen with despair. Teeth clenched. He kissed his boy on the head.

There was no answer. The boy's shivering stopped. Complete silence.

"Listen to me! Where is Cheng? Is he dead!—" PaNou demanded.

"PaNou, I beg you! Stop it." Meng begged, tears pouring like a broken faucet.

She clawed one of the boy's shoulders, shaking him. "Tell me! Where—"

"Do not touch my son! Don't you ever touch my son!" Meng pushed her away. "My son is dying, and all you care about is your Cheng! Have some heart, why don't you!"

PaNou collapsed to the ground. She looked left. Right. All around. The rest of the villagers surrounded them. Many angry eyes blazed at her.

"Your Cheng left with the second group. He wasn't with my son, so stop demanding news from him. They're probably all dead by now! It's better than living through this hell!" Meng kissed Lue's hair, and he and his wife mourned.

"Get out of here, you widow!" Someone from the crowd yelled.

Distraught, she crawled out and distanced herself.

"Get up. Why are you crawling like a dog?" Another woman said.

PaNou rose but clambered on all fours again and struggled to stand. Eyes blurred, she scrambled past the crowd and ran. When her knees started to buckle, she stopped. She gazed hazily at the long skinny dirt road that led into the village—and saw a flash of how excited she and Cheng once were on their first arrival. *Cheng! Why have you gone so long?* Flustered and dizzied, she crashed into the wrong house and was shouted out.

Finally, the mark of two long years came and a surge of energy ignited. It was a feeling like the first time Cheng and PaNou met—an endless oomph of joy and anticipation. PaNou prepared the most flamboyant meal for Cheng's return. After an intensive search, she bought him the

153

exquisite handmade knife that he had always wanted. The tough leather on the handle was reminiscent of his hands.

With the food sitting in the kitchen and the knife in her hands, she sat, waiting by the door. Days turned to weeks. Weeks became months. The arc on her lips diminished. A severe pain collected inside her heart, numbing her entire body. PaNou never touched the large meal and it rotted. Its sweet smell decayed into a thick vinegary stench. The odor kept her awake throughout the entire night. And like the decaying meal, her spirit faded.

Each arriving figure that appeared from the horizon brought hope, but within seconds, PaNou was able to determine from how the individual walked that it wasn't her Cheng. He had always walked with his left shoulder lower than his right and slightly slid his right foot behind him. Her patience crumbled. She stared—detesting the Sky for the promise they had made.

Many months passed. She persisted. More news arrived that additional Hmong soldiers have been killed in combat. The only good news was when nothing was reported. When the dead bodies stopped arriving for many months, PaNou became hysterical at missing the habitual arrivals of corpses. She cursed herself upon realization that her insensible state had been waiting and expecting Cheng's dead body, rather than seeing him return home alive.

The war was much more complex and longer than anyone had predicted, and so the Americans once again asked for more help from the Hmong. Hmong men from other villages had also joined in the war—for there was no turning back for the Hmong people.

PaNou's armor of hope began to crumble, revealing the fragile remains of her love.

The same group of courting men returned. This time reenergized. They courted PaNou like a horde of buzzing flies. Determined, each one had his own method of trying to persuade PaNou that her husband was dead. After all, three years had passed. And she had only heard from Cheng once.

One of the more experienced men admired her unparalleled loyalty.

A bald, dark-skinned man with large floppy ears walked to the front door. He smiled, revealing four missing front teeth. PaNou sat frozen inside the door, looking out.

"I've never seen anyone so loyal and loving to their husband," said the man. Each time he spoke, his sour breath reached her before his words. PaNou had acclimated herself to bad odors, but his was over the stratosphere. It ignited her temper.

"It's called love." PaNou spoke without giving him a look. "Something that you don't have for your wives."

"Well, I have to commend your perseverance, PaNou, but something troubles me. Really, how much longer can you wait?" The man walked, circling like a wolf staring down its prey. "He's dead by now. I also lost my brother. We'll be lucky to see their ashes. You need to move on." He stopped pacing and watched for a reaction.

There was a long pause from the stoical wife.

"PaNou, I understand exactly what you're going through."

PaNou wanted to say, "No, you don't. You have no idea." but it was useless. All the man was doing was reminding her of how much she loathed other men.

"Hey, it took me a long time to get over the loss of my brother. I never had a chance to say goodbye—we never heard of him again. No news means death." He began rubbing the back of his bald head. "Listen, PaNou, life is about living, not about death. To live is to move on. Sometimes you need someone to help you move forward." The old man stroked his chin, hiding a smile. "All I ask of you is if I can help you move forward?"

I don't want to move on.

Still, there was not a word, not even a physical response from PaNou.

"PaNou, you can't keep this up forever. How much longer will it take for you to realize that he won't be coming back?"

Then PaNou's eyes reddened like the setting sun. Finally, she shifted not toward the man but to the door. "We both promised to the Sky. He said two years."

"My goodness! It's been over three years." The old man cheered.

"Has it? I knew it was a little past two—" PaNou's shoulders fell forward.

"PaNou, if he loved you, he would've never left you like this. He betrayed you. If it was me, I'd be a man of my word." He spoke rapidly with enthusiasm. Aware that his words were penetrating, he continued, "Come live with me and you'll never have to work again but watch our kids. I'll take care of you. These are my words—I'll never ever leave you."

The frozen cracks on her forehead began to move like tectonic plates. The man's words were a reminder time had passed.

Denial and anger rushed in. PaNou snapped. She turned to the visitor and cussed him out with the nastiest words imaginable—including the other men who were waiting outside the house.

"Get out! Get your filthy face out of my house before I kill you!" PaNou pulled out the knife she bought for Cheng. "And, if you or your ugly friends ever come here again, I'll cut all of you and feed you to the dogs!"

Those in the back witnessed this and took off running all together. For the devoted PaNou, she didn't want to acknowledge that it had been over two years. However, as the man mentioned, three years had indeed gone by. She then pointed to the Sky, blaspheming it.

"Sky, I trusted you to watch over him. You lied! How could you be so cruel to me?" PaNou started slashing the pole by the entrance until she dropped the long knife, and then she hid her face between her hands.

The lone wife dragged herself to the back of the house. PaNou climbed onto the bamboo stool, lower than ever before. Then, like a breaking storm, emotions unleashed. Shivering nonstop, PaNou wailed. The remaining fluids in her body gushed out in uncontrollable phases. The sporadic thoughts of her beloved husband's death crippled her. That evening she became ill. Lying on her bed, PaNou grabbed the end of her husband's sash, which she wore, sniffed it and squeezed it against her face.

"Honey, why aren't you home yet? You said two years. Please come home and kick these wolves out of our home."

PaNou had trouble breathing. A cold sweat coated her, followed by violent coughing. She pulled against her shirt. Nights passed and her condition worsened. Then, PaNou retrieved some of the money she had stashed away and knew that in each Hmong village, there was at least one medicine woman. PaNou staggered out.

Tong Shia: Home Sweet Home

Four lengthy years passed. At last, Cheng returned home. For his valiant and extended service, Cheng was given a horse to reach home. The war was ongoing, but he had served twice his term and was paid abundantly for it. If managed well, the lump payment was enough to last a lifetime in their simple lifestyle. Exhausted, yet Cheng was more anxious than ever to break the news to PaNou.

For Cheng, he had lost track of time but knew over two years had passed. He kicked his horse to hurry home. As he neared Tong Shia, the picture of his wife's sharp almond eyes and that smile, the only smile that could light an entire room made the journey only longer. He couldn't wait to park his hands on her round hips—for that was where home truly was.

In the late and quivering night, Cheng confronted the hazy village. He stopped at the hilltop. From there it was downhill to the valley where a night mist blanketed Tong Shia. He hesitated briefly. Something about the village looked and felt different—gloomier than what he remembered.

This is the right place.

The half moon, its lustrous orange-yellow color stalked over the village like a single squinting eye.

A cold breeze rattled his spine. Cheng rubbed his eyes, scanning his memory twice to make certain it was the right village. He shifted his buttocks slightly because they were numb from the long bouncy ride. The jingling of his bag moved him forward. His horse trotted further until they were fifty yards from the first house. Abruptly, the horse neighed and jumped in the opposite direction. Cheng pulled and straightened the stallion's head with the reins, but it fought back. For five long seconds it was a tug-a-war and his stallion nearly threw him off. Displeased, Cheng gave the horse a heavy and loud slap in the rear, reminding it who was master.

Upon approaching closer, he recognized their leaning boxy house. A smile broke. Cheng dismounted from the saddle and forcibly pulled his horse behind the house, tying it to a wooden pole. He observed how quiet the town was.

I missed you so much. His heart widened a hundred miles across.

Cheng felt another frigid gust of wind that crept from the bottom of his tailbone, up his spine, and crashed at the nape of his neck. He shivered and crossed his hands under his armpits. The puffing sounds of his exhausted horse died out behind him. The yearning husband ceased his steps. He examined the once-familiar atmosphere. Again, the tinkling coins pressed him forward.

With a surge of zeal, he declared softly, "Sweetheart, from today on our life will be completely different."

A sputtering sound raced across from the left side, out of Meng's house and into his. Such sound silenced the horse. He looked up and saw the last frame of a four-legged shadow.

"Chance! Come here, boy!" Cheng knelt down clapping his thighs. "Stupid dog! What a waste of food." Cheng was never fond of that dog. He knew better than to expect it to obey him. It rarely did anyway. There were times when Cheng wondered if Meng had given him the dog so he would have one less dog to feed. As much as he looked forward to seeing PaNou, he also wanted to see Meng as well.

The closer Cheng came to the door, the louder his heart hammered against his rib cage. After being gone for such a long time, he was a bit nervous, wondering how much PaNou had changed physically. Exhausted, Cheng lifted his heavy boots toward the front door. The damp air and eerie quietness gave life to his other senses. Then it dawned on him that the familiar rustling feathers of his chickens and the grunts of his pigs were nowhere to be heard. Even the warm stench of chicken and pig manure was absent.

"This *is* the right place." Cheng reassured himself, looking around. He squeezed his bag.

For a brief moment, Cheng felt like he was walking into someone else's house until he saw the tilted door with two holes. Such marks could not be mistaken, and they welcomed him home.

Can't wait to see you, Sweetheart! He felt extremely fortunate he had returned without losing a limb. Glancing upward at the foggy night sky, he gave a nod to say, "Thank you!" to the Sky.

Cheng didn't want to startle PaNou, so he reached out his knuckles and threw four knocks on the lockless door. No answer. He swallowed a deep breath. Knocking louder, he waited for that warm and affectionate voice he dreamed of every night. Only the deadening silence answered back. Then, right before his dry lips unlocked to call PaNou, a breeze pushed the door and it screeched a few inches inward.

A tailwind whistled, straightening every strand of hair on his body. Cheng brushed the feeling aside. War, with its grotesque and shocking images, had caught up to him. Cheng remembered well what his recruiter told him on the second day: "War will change you more than you change war."

As the moon's light crept to the family room, instantly he recognized the shadow of his favorite bamboo stool. Without hesitation, Cheng jumped on it. The smooth texture of the bamboo cupped his buttocks perfectly—a further confirmation that it was his house.

"Sweetheart! Sweetheart!" Cheng exclaimed while unclipping the numerous pockets of the bag.

Only silence answered back.

She must be asleep. As the cash and coins rained and jingled to the floor, Cheng's grin widened.

A disheveled sound brushed against the back wall where it was mostly dark. Suddenly, a tall shadow slid from the opposite corner, terrifying every ounce of life from him.

"Sweetheart!" Cheng flinched. "You nearly gave me a heart attack." The war had gotten him very jumpy. With effort, Cheng regained his composure and stood, ready to hug and embrace PaNou, his devoted wife. "Do you know how much I've missed you—"

"No!" she shouted. Her voice was deeper than he remembered, and shaky. "I have a bad fever. I'm not feeling good at all. Don't want you to catch it."

"All right." Cheng sat down, somewhat hurt, but understanding. "Gosh, I missed you so much." He turned his attention to the bag. "You wouldn't believe how much money we have now."

Cheng waited for a loving response from PaNou. The seconds of silence passed like hours. Cheng rubbed his eyes for a better look. Except for the tiny strands of dim moonlight peering through cracks and holes, the shadows in the corner made it hard to see PaNou. She began to walk closer toward the thin rays. Cheng recognized the figure, the shape, and most of all, the long silky hair.

Cheng held the large bag up like a trophy. "I told you I was coming back. Our life will be so much better—"

"What took you so long? I thought you were as good as dead." PaNou loomed closer, dragging herself to the center of the room.

"Oh, that's war, Sweetheart. It's never finished until too many people die—"

"You've made me wait for so, so long."

"I'm very sorry. We didn't have enough men, so I was forced to stay." Cheng began to untie the laces on his big boots. His breathing puffed with a long sigh, followed by sniffles.

"Are you okay?"

He shook his head while shaking dirt out of his boots. "War is not for the faint-hearted. At the beginning, I made a very good friend named, Pheng...then one evening he was standing right next to me as we walked in separate groups through the jungle. We kept walking and it started to rain a lot like that one night when we made our ocean, and then, the forest behind us came alive with bullets. He yelled for me to get down. So I did, and then there was a sudden thud. I looked over and there he was flat on the ground. The side of his head was blown right off. His mouth was still wide open…he didn't even get a chance to finish talking to me," Cheng said, taking a hard swallow.

"You are so lucky…"

Cheng shrugged his shoulders. "It's dark and cold in here. You mind starting a fire, Sweetheart?"

"Do you know you had me worried to death? I missed you very much."

"I missed you, too. But hey, look at us now!" Cheng dumped the remaining cash to the floor. Eyes tightened, he whispered, "I can't wait until I see that *bastard*, Meng." Cheng began sorting the cash.

"I really thought you weren't coming back."

"Sweetheart, I'm very sorry, okay. I *feel* terrible. It's like one minute we stop to rest, next minute we have to go. I wrote you as often as I could."

"Really? As often as you could and that was only one letter."

"What, one letter? I sent at least twenty letters, each with money."

"Never got them. Are you just saying this to make me happy?"

"No! My goodness!" Cheng held a fist in one hand. "They took the money. A lot of money. I should've known, but I had no other way. Anyway, our future is what matters now. Good thing I kept this. We'll still be fine."

"Is it always about money?"

"No. It's about life. Happiness. No more begging others."

"Well, I wasn't happy. You said two years…you promised me." PaNou coughed a hissing sound. "You—"

"Sweetheart, we're all going to catch a cold in here. Can you please start a fire?" Cheng remembered the oath but wanted to change the subject. The last thing he wanted upon coming home was an argument. "I'll get you some medicine first thing tomorrow morning."

Out of nowhere, Cheng inhaled something nauseating. He grabbed his throat and tried coughing it out.

"What is that nasty smell?" Cheng grimaced.

"I-I buried Chance under our bed."

"You *buried* that dog under our bed?" Cheng echoed her words back in shock. "But I thought I just saw…never mind," said Cheng, fatigued. "Dang it! Must be one of Meng's stupid dogs running around again." *Some things never change.* The death of Chance saddened him, though they never bonded. Worse, burying a dog under a bed was the craziest thing he had ever heard of.

"Can you get the fire going?" Having to ask her three times, Cheng was losing patience and was about to start his own fire.

"I got it."

Cheng calmed himself. He was avoiding any hint of a quarrel while PaNou was providing every reason to. Weary, Cheng disregarded the topic. He continued to untie his bags. The disgusting odor forced him to spit out his saliva every time he exhaled. "Just…start the fire, please."

PaNou walked over to the back room and piled sticks to the center. The light from the door and walls allowed Cheng to pick up more details. He wanted to see her close again and turned to look while she slithered in and out of the night's shadows. She looked even taller than he remembered. PaNou wore his scarlet sash, but the sash and long skirt were soiled, raggedy, and filthy. Cheng pondered why she hadn't bought any new clothing with the money he had sent. He began to realize that some things had changed over the years. It wasn't only PaNou's attire that was different, but her presence, their home, and Tong Shia. And just as likely, he also had changed. Was he gone too long and had forgotten village life? Forgotten how his wife was?

"It's great to be home." Cheng continued his optimism. "Many times, I swear I could've been killed, yet the Sky protected me. Thank you, Sky." He turned to PaNou. "I love you."

"...love never dies." She whispered in a sudden cracking sound before clearing her throat.

Cheng kept busy organizing his stash. PaNou burnt a match and reached for the small pile of kindling. The fire snapped the sticks but died quickly. This repeated many times until the exhausted husband finally lost his patience.

"Did you forget how to make a fire? You need to blow enough to spread to the rest."

As instructed, PaNou softly blew across the pile of twigs. Each time she puffed, there was a faint but startling sound of popping and cracking. The flame ignited only to die out to popping sounds. When Cheng stopped counting the coins, the disturbing sounds became imminent. The harder she blew, the louder the noise grew. Suddenly, the sporadic sounds froze his spirit. All his senses came alive for the second time. Like a sniper, he zoomed in at the target from the corner of his eyes. There, he saw a waterfall of giant maggots pouring from each side of her lipless mouth. As the flames came back flickering like a strobe light, he witnessed a horrendous scene beyond his nightmares: PaNou's entire face was purplish white. The flesh below her eyes was gone and so were her eyelids. The only thing holding her lower jawbone together was drooping skin. A gap in her sagging cheek revealed the side of a long slithering black tongue, and rotting molars. Cheng's heart almost stopped. In that instant, he could have died ten times over, but he had seen his share of graphic deaths in the war.

With every ounce of life, Cheng managed to restrain from screaming. The terrifying sight a few feet away immediately superseded the brain-exploding, gushing, and splattering scene that haunted Cheng.

A gentle breeze squeezed in from the door to the pile of twigs. Finally, the fire started, and PaNou folded under the cover of the shadows.

A cold sweat layered his forehead. His shrunken heart began to pick up pace again. In a state of shock, he didn't want to believe his senses. Had the carnage of war made him mad? Cheng wanted to check with neighbors. He had to come up with a plan—a quick plan!

"I-I need to pee so badly," Cheng said as calmly as could be. Holding his bladder like it was about to burst, he continued, "The entire trip, I never stopped to rest because I wanted to come home and see you. I-I'll be right back, S-Sweetheart." Cheng had to force every bit of courage to say the last word.

"Promisssse?" Her word penetrated Cheng's soul, and his frightened spirit was about to leave him.

"Of course." He rushed out, nearly tripping over his own legs.

Cheng fought to not fall. He remembered his father's warning while telling him ghost stories as a kid: *If you fall, your spirit will jump out and that's when the monster can snatch you.* While Cheng ran, he watched for rocks, twigs, holes, and anything else that could cause him to trip. He scowled in horror, trying to make sense of what just happened.

Behind the house, Cheng quickly grabbed a large gourd of water and gently tipped it at an angle to simulate peeing. Maybe he's truly gone mad, so he slapped himself to try to wake himself from a nightmare. The slaps burned, confirming his unfortunate reality. He darted to a neighbor's house. No one in sight. For some strange reason, the neighbors had left everything, including sandals, pots, and clothing as if they were still present. Time was running out. He rushed to Meng's place. Exact same scenario. There were no signs of his best friend's rowdy dogs either. Dumbfounded, Cheng's tired mind raced in full gear, trying to conclude what had happened.

Cheng could not come to peace with what he witnessed inside his house, and wished it to be a bizarre trick of imagination. He tried convincing himself that maybe the enemy had raided the village. It was the only logical explanation for the entire village to be deserted like this. Yet, there was no trace of bloodshed or fighting.

The shaken husband slowed his running. At once, Cheng raised his hand to the Sky and begged for forgiveness. As if reacting to Cheng's prayer, the clouds began to cover the luminous moon.

On Cheng's way back, a strip of paper blew by his foot. It danced and spun around, begging for attention. He reached down and picked it up. The paper carried a heavy load of emotion as it read:

The love that Mrs. Cheng Yang had for her husband was genuine and irreplaceable. For the death of her beloved husband, Cheng Yang, she had poisoned herself and left us. For death will bring Mr. and Mrs. Cheng Yang together, forever.

Cheng's spirit nearly shattered its shell—his body broke into a relentless tremble.

"PaNou...my sweetheart, my life. I am so sorry. If you can hear me, please forgive me," Cheng cried to the Sky.

"Cheng?" The once-sweet voice returned from the house.

Cheng cowered.

"What's taking you so long?"

He heard a soft voice that was PaNou's mixed with a spine-breaking growling tone.

Cheng sprinted behind the house, saddled his horse, and took off as quickly as possible. It wasn't until he was up the first hill that he remembered his hoard of cash. *AHHH! CRAP!* Cheng's mind screamed. He couldn't go back. He didn't want to. Not after what he saw. Cheng bit his lip and he kicked the horse forward.

No regret. No going back. Cheng reminded himself of his life's motto. It was to make him feel better about the money and his grim life. It wasn't working. *Why didn't I stick some money into my pockets!*

Shortly after, the figure inside charged out—only to witness an empty gourd. Upset, she smashed the gourd against a large pail, clattering it against the house. Slouched over on all hairy fours, she dug her hind legs into the dirt, licked the floor, and lunged after his sweaty scent.

Cheng turned back and saw the four-legged creature in the distance. His shoulders tensed and his face cringed upon realization: *That shadow I saw running over to my house, that wasn't Chance. It was that monster!*

Cheng rode his horse up and down the beautiful terrain, but there was not a moment to savor the scenery. His heart raced with each stride. Cheng was kicking the horse's ribs and slapping its rear so hard he was damaging the already weakened stallion. In fact, he nearly heeled it to death.

The sun was making its way up the eastern horizon, while a hefty shadow bounced after him—growing larger with each leap. After a few miles, the stallion showed its exhaustion from the previous trip, and also from Cheng's current abuse. One hill led to another hill—he didn't remember so many hills before! The quick descents and ascents wore out the horse. Cheng threw heavier kicks. Downhill was a matter of maintaining balance as Cheng leaned back so the stallion didn't tumble frontward. By the last and fifth hill, Cheng could crawl faster uphill than the beaten horse.

With the sun peeking behind his back, the shadowy figure pounced closer and disappeared between the first and second hills. There was no way he or the snail-speed horse could outrun the dreadful creature. Cheng stopped the horse. Hopped off.

Adrenaline actually made Cheng smarter and more analytical than his frightened state earlier. Something he learned he had a skill for: survival. Cheng looked back to the hill he had just passed. Less than twenty yards from the road, stood a dead strangler fig tree of colossal size. Ancient in its latticework and buttressed trunk, it had enormous vines wrapping around it like anacondas. There was a large vertical opening on the northwest side of its massive bark. Cheng knew his only chance of survival was to hide inside.

The shadow loomed ever closer. He took off his shirt, paused at it, at his only shirt that had been a part of him like a longtime friend. Cheng quickly tied it to the reins and slapped the exceedingly fatigued horse to trot away. The horse almost crashed on its trembling legs. One more slap would've killed it. Cheng darted toward the tree. The tree towered over him with its long outstretched branches. It looked no different than a skeletal frame of an enormous monster with multiple arms.

Cheng climbed inside.

Nooks and crannies throughout the hollow tree emitted light inside and revealed its spacious canals. Immediately, he fell on his knees, praying, pleading to the Sky to forgive him. Cheng prayed so loud his voice shook the inner walls—and without knowing, interrupted the slumber of an oversized feline with two kittens. Before he finished his prayer, a muscular bluish-black jaguar snarled its glowing white fangs. Its yellow eyes illuminated from above, hovering like a pair of full moons. Its sticky saliva dripped on Cheng's forehead. The gooey fluid warmed the side of his cheek.

For Cheng, he'd rather be eaten by the jaguar than by the monster chasing him. Nevertheless, Cheng begged the provoked cat to spare him.

The feline's hide straightened, doubling its size. Two kittens yelped from above. Swiftly, the enraged cat jumped, soaring over Cheng to the opposite sidewall. It sniffed the air erratically. Sensing a stronger odor arriving, the feline dismissed the less-threatening presence in Cheng.

Cheng scrambled up the channel as fast as he could. With each leg against the opposite walls, he kicked and bounced higher. Looking down between his split legs that kicked into the rugged walls, he continued his prayer. A minute later, the rumbling of a bulky body dashed past the tree. A sense of relief overcame him. Worn out, he breathed life again and began climbing down—stopping when he heard a quick cry of his distant horse. Then silence. With haste, Cheng kicked up the tree again.

In a short time, something heavy lurked toward the tree; it began rubbing against the bark. It sniffed the dirt in a half circle to the trunk. Something massive tore inside. Its deep breathing shook the walls of the tree. Despite being only half the size of the enormous dark intruder, the jaguar growled at it to leave.

"He'zzzz here. I can szzzmmell hizzz fleszzzzh." A demonic voice thundered the inner canals of the tree. There was still a hint of PaNou's sweet voice in the back of the roar.

The two kittens opposite Cheng yelped louder. The fresh smell of horse blood tainted the air.

The enraged cat growled back, deafening the cries of its babies. With its blazing steel-like claws projected, it pounced on the monstrous intruder without hesitation. They clawed and brawled, followed by ear-piercing shrieks. Meanwhile, Cheng and the kittens hid high in the tree. The kittens whimpered. Their cries diminished Cheng's hope. No one could tell from the fracas below who was winning. Eyes shut, Cheng prayed again.

After two quaking minutes, the screaming and growling came to a dead silence. Frightened, the two kittens clawed themselves to the ceiling. Neither Cheng nor the kittens had the courage to crawl down. Then he heard sharp sounds of teeth crunching on bones. Suddenly, out from the bottom corner of the tree trunk, a head tumbled out and stopped—dark eyes piercing the sky. Dark pearl eyes shimmered with a dim green hue—staring directly into his soul.

Cheng snapped his eyes shut. In the blackness of his eyelids, the two green eyes still glowed in his mind, like the pair he first saw when he followed PaNou and her parents to Lou Sai. A heavy pain entered his heart, and his entire face tightened. Flashbacks of PaNou overcame him: her laughing voice, dancing black hair, and her curvy calves that seduced him from the beginning.

Cheng pounded his chest to breathe. Then he lost his footing and fell to the ground. As he fell over the top of the head, Cheng split his legs in time to avoid stepping on the decapitated head.

The blood-soaked shaggy body of his former wife was battered, cleaved, and tossed against the floor. With a confirmation of triumph, the black jaguar gave a deafening roar.

Cheng drop to his knees to thank the feline family. The jaguar wobbled toward the corpse, followed by its kittens. They began gnawing on the hairy corpse. The large cat growled at Cheng, flaring its canines as if to say, "Get out or we'll have you for dessert!"

Cheng scurried away. He turned to look back—falling more than once to the ground. He ran and ran and ten minutes later, he continued increasing the distance on the rugged trail. By now, the land was an open war, where guerrilla soldiers fought with no boundaries. Down the trail, Cheng slowed down to catch his breath while looking behind him in case there was something else following. Then, in an instant, a group of guerrilla soldiers appeared from the turn of the trail. Their language was foreign to Cheng, and their eyes, their eyes were painted with death—all targeted at Cheng. Like a wild animal, Cheng vanished into the jungle. The soldiers immediately chased him, followed by a series of screaming bullets.

Branches punched, kicked, and whipped Cheng, as he searched deep within himself for another burst of energy to run. The soldiers were closing the distance. Cheng's lungs pulsated in pain with each stride, and each breath sent a burning ache throughout his chest. Then, suddenly, his next step found no ground, only a steep emptiness where Cheng fell, free-falling. Maybe it was only three seconds, but it felt like an eternity until he crashed to the ground, flipped and then there was a loud thud inside his mind.

Cheng woke up to a voice singing; it wasn't just any voice, but a voice that entranced the branches, the birds, and the throbbing pain on the rear corner of his head. Like a snake, he slithered through the tall grass, toward the singing voice. She was Hmong—she was singing *kwv txhiaj*, traditional Hmong love songs that were poetic and heartwarming. Her song rippled long strokes of life into his soul. There, a young Hmong woman dressed in a black shirt with a snow-white skirt sat on a boulder with her torso leaning over the stream. Her long silky hair shimmered in the sunlight. Suddenly, when his senses caught up to him, Cheng became hysterical. He breathed with a short-pitched grunt. The pacing of his grunts increased as he drew nearer. Scenes of the gruesome monster that had chased him earlier, combined with the sudden rush of soldiers shooting, overcame him. His own fingers began to claw his face.

Across the river stood a few houses made from what Cheng was used to seeing in his native village. Blue and green dragonflies swarmed the shore like fairies—many of them hovered around the young woman. She continued washing and singing. Cheng stood behind her and rested his hand on her shoulder. Unlike most people who would scream or be startled, instead she slowly breathed out her last few *kwv txhiaj* lyrics and, frame by frame, turned to look over her shoulder. The side of her face slowly came into sight. Cheng's heavy eyelids lifted. Her left eye came into view— sharp at the ends like an almond, followed by high cheekbones, and ruby lips that Cheng could taste in his own mouth.

"Pa…Nou?"

The End

Ncas

The Ncas, pronounced "njaa," is made of brass and has a bamboo case and string attached at one end.

The "Ncas" or mouth harp is traditionally used by the Hmong in courtship and played by either young men or women. Clever couples can use the instrument as a private form of communication. This instrument can be used to combine the spoken word and verbal tones.

The instrument is played by putting the thin metal blade of the instrument up against and between the upper and lower lips, and plucking the blade to produce vibrations. The vibrations of the blade manipulate the lip and mouth cavity to produce a kind of masked combination of speech and music.

Inhaling and exhaling help produce the sounds of the instrument.

The Hmong People

The Hmong originated in China, and as far north as Siberia over five thousand years ago. An estimated seven to ten million Hmong, also referred to as Miao remain in the southern and western provinces of China, particularly in Hunan, Guizhou, and Yunnan.

For centuries, the Hmong were politically oppressed while they tried to maintain their independence. As a result, some migrated south to Laos, Thailand, Vietnam, and Burma (Myanmar). Their international recognition occurred when they allied themselves with the United States during the Vietnam War in Laos (The Secret War).

Today, there are an estimated 400,000 Hmong in the United States, while others have resettled in Australia, Canada, France, French Guiana, Germany, and other countries.

**For more information about the Hmong People,
here are some sources:**

www.HmongABC.com

www.HmongArchives.org

www.HmongCC.org

About the Author

Patch Xiong was born in 1981 in Laos. At two months old, his family escaped to Thailand where Patch spent his first four and half years in the Ban Vinai Refugee Camp before immigrating to Minnesota.

The sudden loss of his father in 2001 triggered his move to Alaska where he continued school. Xiong holds a computer programming degree from Minneapolis Business College and a business degree from Alaska Pacific University.

Patch is a founding member of Alaska Writer's Guild, an organization dedicated to helping published and unpublished writers.